Skull in the Birdcage

Dedication

David:
Julie, Dave, and AnnaBell

Charlie:
The Kid

Special thanks from the co-authors to Dave Pearson at Sigil Publishing. His dedication and patience are appreciated.

This book is fiction. The people, places, events, and pink-antennaed slithersaurs depicted within are fictitious. Any resemblance to persons living or dead or to real life places is purely coincide and, in all honesty, probably a little disturbing.

ISBN 0-9728461-1-5

Printed in the U.S.A.

First Printing, October 2003

Skull in the Birdcage Contents

The World of Knightscares

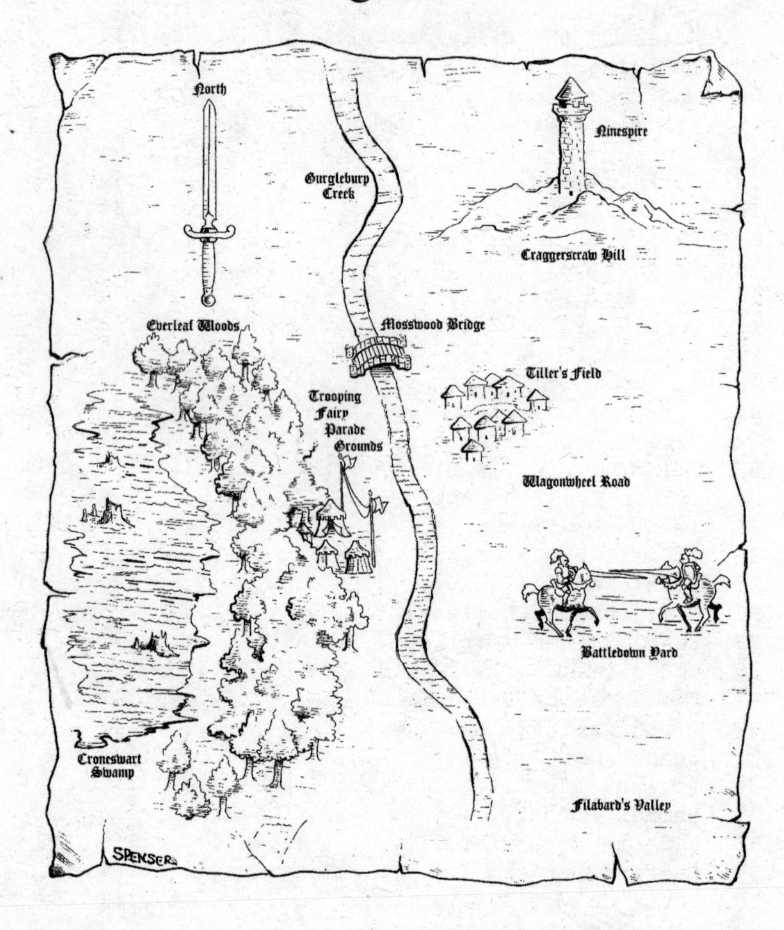

Deephome-Glimmering and Surroundings

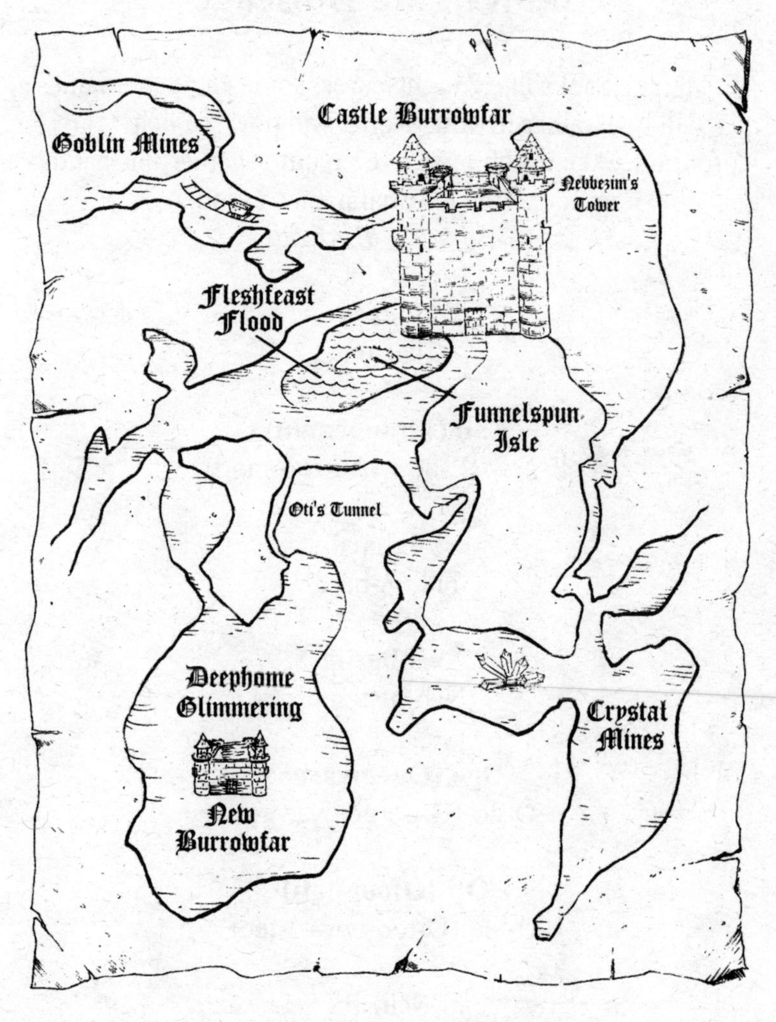

Fantasy Name Guide
for
Skull in the Birdcage

In fantasy books like Knightscares, some character names will be familiar to you. Some will not. To help you pronounce the tough ones, we've put together this handy guide to the unusual names found in *Skull in the Birdcage*.

Charos
Char-ose

Enu (Enunarumu)
E-new (E-new-nah-roo-moo)

Filabard
Fill-uh-bard

Nebbezim
(Neb-beh-zim)

Ogo (Ogogiyargo)
O-go (O-go-gee-yar-go)

Oti (Otoonuoti)
O-tee (O-too-new-o-tee)

Schrat
Rhymes with *rat*, has a *shh* sound at the beginning.

#2

Skull in the Birdcage

David Anthony
and
Charles David

Princess Oti

The Long-Awaited Day

1

As soon as my eyes opened, I jumped out of bed. *Today's the day!* I excitedly reminded myself like I really needed reminding. There wasn't anything that could make me forget.

Yawning, I shook my head irritably. I'd been too excited to sleep last night and I was paying for it. But there was no way I'd let sleepiness slow me down.

I'd turned twelve the week before. The age a kid can become a knight. Well, a page really. A *page* is a knight-in-training or a knight-to-be.

While I've always considered myself a knight, I was about to officially begin training.

I already knew how to ride a horse, carry a lance, and wield a sword. But a knight's training is more than practicing to fight. It's about learning the *Noble Deeds and Duties*. That's every knight's code of behavior. Aside from being strong, brave, and good in battle, a knight must know about honor and justice.

Act Five of the *Noble Deeds and Duties* sums it up:

The Common Good is Best Served by Uncommon Honor.

In other words, a knight must be honorable at all times for the good of everyone. As for the Acts, they're sort of the rules for knighthood. There's one hundred Acts in the *Noble Deeds and Duties.*

I dressed quickly in my best outfit, a dark blue doublet trimmed in black, some blue hose, and a pair of low boots. Checking myself in the mirror, I thought I looked pretty knightly.

My blond hair was cut very short. Most knights wear their hair that way because it gets hot under their helmets. I also thought I looked taller than I had the day before. Maybe I'd had another growing spurt in the night.

"Connor," my father liked to tease me, "stop growing so fast or we'll have to keep you in a barn." He was joking, of course. I wasn't *that* big, and we didn't have a barn.

Following the delicious scent of bacon into the kitchen, I found that my parents had left breakfast for me. They'd left before the sun had risen to prepare for the Turning of the Pages ceremony.

That's where I needed to be by noon. Knights and pages from all over the kingdom would participate. Not just from Tiller's Field where I lived. The ceremony was where and when new pages would be named. It happened only once a year and was a very big deal.

A soft knock on the front door told me that Simon had arrived. Simon was a boy my age who would also be named a page. Only he didn't want to be.

Simon was kind of small, pretty clumsy, and more interested in books and magic tricks than swords and noble deeds. But his father was a knight, too, so Simon didn't have much choice.

I hauled the door open fast to startle him. "Good morning, peasant," I shouted to add to the surprise. I called everyone who isn't a knight "peasant". That included people like Simon who didn't want to be knights.

The *whoosh* of the door along with my loud voice worked perfectly. Simon sputtered in surprise and fumbled the four apples he'd been juggling. One even bounced off his head of floppy red hair.

Juggling was just about the only thing Simon could do that required coordination. So long as he wasn't distracted, that is.

"Good morning," Simon said cheerfully. Nothing much bothered him. Not even an apple bouncing on his head.

"Good morning, *sir*," I corrected. Peasants were supposed to call knights "sir".

Simon shrugged and rolled his eyes. "Whatever you say, *Sir* Bigmouth," he snickered. When I didn't laugh with him, he shrugged again then scooped up his fallen apples.

No, Simon would never be a real knight. But he was a good sport.

Crrrrrunch, Simon bit into one of his apples. "Got anything to eat?" he asked with a mouthful of fruit.

Got anything to eat, sir? I said to myself. But there was no point in saying it out loud. Simon wouldn't change.

I never would have guessed it then, but I'm alive today because of Simon. A whole lot of people are. He's something of a hero. Brave and chivalrous just like a real knight. There's a lot more to him than you'd expect from a clumsy bookworm.

Mr. Sootbeard's Silent Stable

2

Even though my parents had made breakfast for me, Simon ate most of it. I don't know where he put it all. He wasn't a very big kid.

If I ate like him, I really would have to live in a barn!

After breakfast, we cleaned our dishes and left. The Turning of the Pages ceremony would take place outside of town at Battledown Yard. It's also where knights held jousting tournaments. The Yard was a couple of hours east of Tiller's Field, so we'd have to hurry to be there by noon.

Lucky for us I had my own horse, Honormark, a spirited charger. I called him Honormark because of a black mark on his nose that looked like a shield. The rest of his body was white.

The stables were located on the other side of town. On our walk, I decided to ask Simon about something that had been bothering me.

"Why don't you want to be a knight?" I asked. "Are you

happy being a peasant?"

Simon laughed and raised one eyebrow at me. I couldn't do that. Raise just one eyebrow. "You don't really believe all that peasant nonsense, do you?" he asked.

His question made me frown. "Sure I do," I said defensively. "There's royalty, knights, and peasants. In that order. Kings and queens are royalty and they're born that way. So that leaves knights or peasants for the rest of us."

He laughed again. "Can knights or peasants do this?"

With a quick flick of his wrist, he tossed an apple high above his head. It was the same color as his hair. As the apple fell, he brought up his hands to catch it and mumbled something I didn't quite hear.

The apple stopped falling and rotated slowly in mid-air.

"How did…?" I started to ask when Simon hooked his finger at the apple. It shot through the air at an angle and bonked me on the head.

"That's for surprising me when you opened the door," Simon smirked as he held out his hand for me to shake. "Now we're even. Still friends?"

I shook his hand eagerly. I'd deserved getting hit with the apple. It was only fair for what I'd done to him earlier.

As for making the apple float in the air, almost anyone could learn magic tricks. Simon practiced them all the time. It's not like he was a wizard using real magic.

We arrived at the stables a short while later. Mr. Sootbeard the blacksmith has a big barn on his property where most everyone from Tiller's Field keeps their horses.

Strangely, we didn't see or hear Mr. Sootbeard around. He wasn't in his house or in the forge out back. Usually there was smoke coming from the chimney and the clanging of a hammer coming from the forge.

"Maybe he's running an errand," Simon suggested.

"Could be," I agreed half-heartedly, but I knew Mr. Sootbeard better. He wouldn't leave without posting a sign or note. He had the only key to the stable.

Simon suddenly flinched and ducked into a half-crouch. He pointed at the stable. "Someone's inside," he whispered.

The stable door was slightly ajar. That meant that either Mr. Sootbeard was inside or that someone had broken in. Mr. Sootbeard wouldn't leave without locking up.

"Keep quiet and stay down," I said and waved my arm for Simon to follow. We had to find out what was going on. It was the knightly thing to do.

We quietly crept across the yard to the stable and stopped to catch our breath. Pressed up against the wall next to the door, I took a deep gulp then silently mouthed the words "One…two…three."

On *three*, I threw the door open wide and charged inside.

The interior of the stable was dark and strangely quiet. A short row of railed stalls formed a hallway that turned to the right a short distance ahead. The stalls were full of shadows and looked abandoned.

I stopped when I noticed that the gate to the stall on my

left was open. Simon bumped into my back.

"Excuse…" he started to apologize but I waved him off. There was something moving in the stall. Not a horse or Mr. Sootbeard. Something taller than my waist and covered with dark hair.

An angry growl came from the stall and yellow eyes stared out at me from the darkness.

The Scruffy-Looking Knight

3

"Heel, Thorn!" I called urgently, my voice cracking in panic.

Thorn was Mr. Sootbeard's dog, a baron mastiff that guarded his property. The dog was all teeth, muscles, and mean personality. But I couldn't understand why it was lurking in an empty stall.

The mastiff's growl was low and deep as it stalked slowly from the stall. The hackles on its neck stood up straight and its lips curled back in a snarl. Its yellow teeth were as thick as my thumb.

"Thorn," I tried more calmly.

Thorn barked in warning. The familiarity of my voice wasn't having any effect. At least not a good one. I was going to have to defend myself.

A shovel used to clean the stables leaned against the wall next to me. Without taking my eyes from Thorn's, I slowly reached out and grasped its handle.

Thorn dipped his big head and growled deeper, preparing for a fight.

I drew the shovel in front of me and gripped it like a staff in both hands. My mouth went suddenly dry and my heart pounded in my ears like a war drum. I didn't want to hurt Thorn, but the mastiff didn't seem to have any doubts about hurting me or Simon.

As he barked again, I raised the shovel.

"Wait!" Simon gasped from behind me. "*Bravery Without Honor is Cowardice*," he quoted from the *Noble Deeds and Duties*. It was Act Thirty, one I could never really figure out.

How could being brave make someone a coward?

Before I had time to wonder about what it meant, Simon stepped around me and knelt in front of Thorn. He stretched out a shaking hand toward the mastiff's nose and its vicious teeth.

Thorn stopped advancing but kept growling. Drool streamed from his jaws.

"*Thorrrnnn*," Simon purred soothingly. His hand lightly touched the dog's quivering muzzle. "Down, boy. Sit."

Thorn's yellow eyes stared at Simon, and for a brief second, I got a sense that Thorn wanted nothing more than to sink his teeth into Simon's hand. But instead, the mastiff whimpered quietly and dropped onto its stomach.

I sighed in relief and heard Simon do the same. He playfully scratched Thorn's broad head.

"Something frightened him," he said thoughtfully. "He wouldn't normally threaten us, right?"

I shook my head vigorously back and forth. "No, never. He knows me. He's only supposed to act that way when danger is near."

Simon leaped to his feet. His face was white with fear. "Something's in here," he breathed so quietly that I almost couldn't hear him. "Something that scares Thorn."

Nodding, I clutched the shovel more tightly. My mouth was still dry but my hands were sweating. Fear has a way of turning everything upside down.

I inched past Thorn and tried to control my breathing. For some reason, I was panting like I'd just run up a steep hill. My arms and legs felt all wobbly and weak. Simon breathed heavily behind me.

I knew that whatever could scare Thorn would be terrifying to us.

The Test of True Bravery is to Embrace Fear, I told myself. Act Twenty-four. It meant that only when a knight is genuinely afraid can actions be considered brave. There is nothing heroic about doing something that doesn't make a knight at least a little bit frightened.

I repeated the Act silently as we crept down the passage. Straw and dirt crunched under our boots, and our heavy breathing echoed in the narrow corridor. Whatever waited ahead would surely hear us coming.

Just as we were about to turn the corner, someone

shouted a loud "Yah!" from farther back in the stable. It was a scratchy voice like a person with a really bad sore throat.

"Look out!" I yelled and threw myself into Simon. We crashed into a gate and tumbled into the stall just in the nick of time.

Honormark, my horse, charged around the corner in a gallop. His eyes were wide and his nostrils flared. On his back crouched an unshaven man wearing a long, blood red cape.

They raced past us without a glance. If we hadn't fallen into the stall, we'd have been trampled.

I was back on my feet in a rush, charging after Honormark and the thief-of-a-rider. "Come back here," I demanded. "That's my horse!"

The scruffy rider burst through the stable door and pulled up rein. In the sunlight outside I saw that he had squinty eyes and a big, hooked nose like a bird's beak. He wore a double-bladed axe strapped to his back and a dull black breastplate.

When I caught up to him, I pointed at Honormark. "That's my horse," I gasped out of breath. I was too angry to be afraid.

The man sneered at me and laughed. "King's business, peasant," he rasped at me.

"Peasant?" I blurted furiously. This man didn't know that he was talking to a knight!

He threw back his cape and pointed at the insignia on his left shoulder. It was the king's crest. A red rose draped over a golden crown. Only the highest ranking knights wore that symbol.

The thief must be one of the king's personal knights.

My jaw dropped and the man laughed at me again. With a vicious kick, he spurred Honormark into a trot. "The king thanks you for your generosity, peasant," the thieving knight called arrogantly from over his shoulder.

Then he was gone in a cloud of dust from under Honormark's hooves.

Turning of the Pages

4

I hate feeling helpless.

Knights are supposed to be strong and able to defend themselves. But I hadn't been able to stop the scruffy-looking knight from stealing my horse. To him I was just some dopey kid. A nobody.

A peasant.

I threw my arms up in frustration and stared in the direction Honormark and the rider had gone. Toward the eastern side of town. It was the same way Simon and I needed to go to reach the Turning of the Pages ceremony.

"Let's find Sheriff Logan," Simon suggested. Deep in my thoughts, I'd almost forgotten he was there.

I turned sharply on my heels. Normally I'd go straight to the sheriff to report a crime. It's his job to track down criminals.

Only I had somewhere extremely important to be. I couldn't afford to spend the time it would take to find the sheriff and explain what had happened. If Simon and I wanted to reach Battledown Yard by noon, we'd have to hurry.

I grabbed Simon by the sleeve and turned him to the stable. "Come on," I told him, "we have to find another horse or we won't make it in time."

"But isn't that stealing?" Simon protested. "Act Seven—*Use Only That Which is Earned or Freely Given.*"

For someone who didn't want to be a knight, he sure knew a lot about the *Noble Deeds and Duties*.

"Well, it would be," I explained, "if we were really going to steal a horse. But we aren't. We're going to borrow one."

Simon started to object but I cut him off. I knew he wanted to remind me that borrowing without permission was almost as bad as stealing. But he didn't know that I had permission to borrow this horse.

Last summer, my friends Josh and Jozlyn rescued our town after everyone had been turned into frogs. Afterward, they'd been rewarded. Josh became Sheriff Logan's deputy and Jozlyn was named apprentice to a good witch. An *apprentice* is like a student who learns all there is to know about one subject.

Jozlyn is very busy learning about magic. As a favor, she'd asked me to exercise her horse Zippity. So whenever I visited Honormark, I took Zippity for a little ride, too.

I'd take Zippity for a little bit longer ride, that's all.

I explained this to Simon. He seemed unsure but decided to go along with me. He didn't want to walk all the way to Battledown Yard any more than I did. It would take hours longer than riding.

We found Zippity in her stall munching lazily on some hay. She was a chubby, brown mare with white socks. Calling her Zippity was kind of funny. Zipping usually means moving fast, but Zippity was anything but fast. I think she thought of herself as a cow instead of a horse.

Even with both of us riding her we made good time. We quickly left town and followed Wagonwheel Road toward the jousting yard. A glance overhead told me that we had two hours before the ceremony started. Just enough time if we hurried.

I started to get excited again and forgot about the scruffy knight who'd stolen Honormark. Simon and I would be knights. Everything else would turn out all right.

Riding behind me, Simon broke our silence. "Bring anything to eat?" he asked.

I almost fell out of the saddle. How could he be hungry again? "You can't be serious!" I exclaimed. "We just had breakfast."

Simon fidgeted. "Well…maybe a snack. We've got a big day ahead."

"But you don't even want to be a knight," I replied.

"Maybe not for my whole life," he admitted, "but while I am, I'm going to try as hard as I can. And to do that, I need a full stomach!" He chuckled and shoved my back playfully.

We both laughed at that, and I thought about what he'd said as we rode. His words made me think of Act Eighteen:

In All Things, Both Noble and Common, Strive Toward Excellence.

Simon might not want to be a knight, but he still planned on being a good one.

That attitude can help out in lots of places. In school, work, and even chores. I know when I try my best at something, I usually don't have to do it twice.

When the sun was almost overhead, we reached Battledown Yard. Knights, horses, and soon-to-be pages crowded the long, grassy field. Flags bearing the king's colors waved from tall poles. Banners depicting scenes of famous battles hung from a large grandstand where the real knights and spectators sat.

I spotted my father among them and waved, but I don't think he saw me. He was reading from a long scroll and frowning.

Simon and I tethered Zippity then hurried to find a seat on the grass in front of the grandstand. We sat on the track where the jousting competitions took place.

Normally an audience would watch from the grandstand but not today. Today dozens of kids crowded around us on the grass waiting excitedly to be named pages.

"This is it," I beamed at Simon. I was so excited that I couldn't keep from smiling.

Simon nodded and swallowed. He looked nervous. "Sure is," he said quietly.

The Turning of the Pages began with a great blowing of trumpets. People all around us cheered and whooped for several minutes. I cheered right along with them. Simon hardly breathed.

The noise died down when two older pages on the grand-stand stepped forward. They carried polished lances with flags tied to their tips, waving them back and forth. The trumpets blared again.

A group of knights in shining armor came forward next. My father was one of them. The group stopped at the edge of the grandstand and my father looked over the field.

"Today," he told us in his deep voice, "is the day you have waited for."

The crowd erupted in more cheering, whistling, and clapping.

My father raised his hands to ask for silence. "But it is my sad duty to inform you...." He cleared his throat and glanced at someone behind him. "It is my sad duty to inform you that there will be no ceremony today."

A gasp went through the crowd. Then there was a heavy silence.

"Please welcome Sir Filabard, Knight of the King's Right Hand," my father announced, turning to the man behind him. "He will explain the necessity for today's cancellation."

I gasped again when Sir Filabard brushed past my father to address the crowd. I recognized his bird-like nose and scruffy face.

Sir Filabard was the man who'd stolen my horse.

Yes?

5

My mind whirled with questions and shock. If I hadn't been sitting, I'd have dropped to the ground like a rock. As it was, my mouth fell open and my stomach tightened.

I felt numb. Everything was going so wrong. There would be no Turning of the Pages and I wouldn't become a knight.

I shook my head and stared in disbelief at scruffy Sir Filabard. King's Right Hand or not, I didn't like him one bit.

Sir Filabard didn't seem concerned. He gripped the railing along the grandstand and leaned forward, squinting down at us with his beady eyes. He looked like a greedy vulture perched over a corpse.

"Greetings," he rasped in his scratchy voice. "You were hoping today would turn out differently, yes?"

A murmur of sad agreement spread through the crowd. Every single one of us was heartbroken. Even Simon.

Sir Filabard shrugged with a sneer. He seemed to enjoy sharing his sad news. As he spoke, he toyed with an hour-glass-shaped ring on his finger. Its blood-red gem sparkled as he twisted the ring round and round.

"To that I say grow up, children," he scolded. "There are more important things to worry about. Indeed, the king is in danger and needs your help. Who here would put his or her concerns above those of our king? To do so would be treason, yes?"

Sir Filabard paused to give us time to think, but no one even dared to breathe. The word treason frightened every-one speechless. It was the worst crime of all. Being accused of it meant never serving the king and never be-coming a knight.

Smirking, the scruffy knight continued to twist his ring. "I'd hoped you would agree. You are all loyal subjects to the crown, and as such, it is your duty to defend the king during times of crisis, yes?"

Everyone fidgeted nervously. "Is it not your duty?" he demanded impatiently.

"Aye, sir!" a girl to my left shouted enthusiastically, and then more voices cried out in support after her.

"We're with you, sir!" cheered a boy I couldn't spot.

"It is our duty!" called another.

"Our privilege, Sir Filabard!" added someone else.

No one else seemed to notice, but I had the feeling that Sir Filabard wasn't what he claimed to be. Real knights didn't steal horses or cancel the Turning of the Pages. And they certainly didn't frighten people by throwing around the word *treason*.

Sir Filabard was up to no good. Why couldn't anyone else see that?

"Excellent, excellent!" he said when the crowd quieted down. "I am pleased to see so many loyal subjects willing to serve the king. To lay down their lives even, yes?"

This time when Sir Filabard paused, the crowd cheered at the top of their lungs. They whistled and clapped. Some even had tears in their eyes.

Smiling smugly, Sir Filabard raised his arms in a call for silence. He looked like a person who had just checkmated an opponent in a game of chess. The hourglass on his finger sparkled in the sunlight.

"To horse then, brave defenders of the crown," he urged. "The king is under attack by an army of goblins. We must defend him at all cost. With our very lives if need be!"

Stunned, my mind whirled again and I stumbled weakly into Simon. Instead of celebrating and being named pages, we were being sent into battle without weapons, armor, or training. Couldn't anyone else see the insanity in that?

But in the eyes of the people around me, I saw only determination and trust. They were all ready to die for Sir Filabard.

Forsake None in Need

6

"Simon, what's going on?" I grabbed him roughly by the shoulders and shook him. The Turning of the Pages had been cancelled and Sir Filabard was marching us off to war. It was unreal.

Simon shook his head and mumbled. He looked as confused as I felt.

Why didn't anyone else seem to care about what was happening?

"I'm going to find my father," I told Simon and climbed to my feet. People scurried this way and that, packing gear and saddling horses. I had to push my way through the crowd.

My father stood on the grandstand talking with a group of other knights. When he finished his conversation, he turned to me with a frown. "I'm sorry your day turned out this way, Connor," he apologized. "It's not what you'd hoped."

I shook my head in frustration. He didn't understand. I

was upset about the ceremony being cancelled, but that wasn't the biggest problem on my mind.

Right then I was worried about goblins. A whole army of them.

Armed with a good sword, I was sure I could handle a goblin one-on-one. Goblins were weak and lazy and never thought of much besides food.

I wasn't worried about fighting. I was worried about *why* we had to fight.

Why was Sir Filabard ordering a bunch of kids into battle? Even counting the few dozen knights who'd been sitting on the grandstand, all of us together didn't make up an army.

I looked my father in the eyes and shook my head again. "It's not the ceremony," I tried to explain. "It's Sir Filabard. He's..."

My father nodded the way a teacher does when you ask an easy question. "Yes, son, I know," he smiled. "Sir Filabard is a great man and valiant knight. His speech has excited us all. We'll be happy to fight and die for him."

Die for him! I repeated in silent horror. Next he'd tell me that sending kids to fight armed with pillows and chicken wings was a perfectly good idea.

I sighed. There was no talking to him right now. He was just as confused by Sir Filabard's speech as everyone else. Everyone but Simon and I, it seemed.

I gave up on looking to him for help. "Your orders, sir?"

I asked with a crisp salute.

My father returned the gesture with a smile. "Stay close to Simon," he advised. "Watch each other's back and listen carefully to Sir Filabard. If anyone can lead us to victory, it's him."

My heart hurt but I nodded anyway. "I won't disappoint you, sir," I promised, only I didn't mean it the way he thought I did.

Simon was sitting in the same spot where I'd left him. I doubted that he'd moved. He stared at the ground with a blank look on his face.

"Come on," I said, "we'd better find Zippity and get ready to leave."

Simon's head shot up in alarm. "You mean to go through with this crazy plan?"

Helplessly, I shrugged. "What choice do we have?"

Simon exhaled loudly. "We don't, I guess. You're right. *Forsake None in Need*, right?" he quoted. It was Act Forty-three and meant that a knight must never abandon anyone who needed help.

Just as we were about to mount up and join the others, a large man appeared from the crowd and strode briskly toward us. He was a knight, but not one I recognized. He wore a great two-handed sword over his shoulder.

"Pardon me, young sirs," he growled with a smirk, and I got the idea that he was privately making fun of us. "I bear a message from Sir Filabard."

I swallowed hard without thinking and the big knight smirked again.

"Sir Filabard is watching you," he warned and then leaned close enough to be heard in a whisper. "And so am I." Then he turned and stalked back into the crowd.

Goblins!

7

"Do you know what that means?" Simon breathed quietly. "Sir Filabard suspects that we don't trust him."

I nodded. "We'll have to pretend until we figure out what's going on," I replied.

There wasn't anything else we could do. We had to act like we believed in Sir Filabard. If he thought we were his enemies, there was no telling what he would do to us.

For the rest of the day and into the evening, we rode south with Sir Filabard in the lead. We crossed rolling hills and passed dozens of farmhouses.

I couldn't understand why we didn't head north toward the king's castle but decided against asking anyone. People might have gotten suspicious if I'd asked questions.

The sun had set and it was dark when we finally stopped in a shallow valley ringed by trees on all sides. The way the trees towered above us made the valley seem darker and deeper than it should.

The fact that we weren't anywhere near the king didn't seem to bother anyone. They acted like this was exactly the place we were supposed to be.

"Make camp!" Sir Filabard shouted down from the rim of the valley. In the darkness I knew him by his raspy voice. When he gave the order, I saw his red ring sparkle in the moonlight.

Senior knights passed out blankets and tents. I didn't see my father and hoped nothing had happened to him.

"Sleep well, young sirs," a familiar voice whispered from behind Simon and me when we'd finished putting up our tent.

We wheeled around to see the big knight that had threatened us before leaving Battledown Yard. He was sitting on a rock with his huge sword on his knees. In one hand he held a whetstone that he swiped up the long blade of his sword.

Whisk, whisk, it went. A *whetstone* is used to sharpen swords and metal tools.

"My tent is right over there," he told us with a nod to our right. His hand swiped the blade again. *Whisk.* "Just in case you…need me." He winked in the most unfriendly way.

Simon stepped forward and met the man's scowl. "We thank you, sir knight," he said with a short bow. He sure was a lot braver than I'd thought.

The big knight grunted and swiped the blade with his

meaty hand again. *Whisk, whisk.* The blade sounded plenty sharp already.

Grabbing Simon's arm, I pulled him into our tent with me. "Why do you think we stopped here?" I asked quietly.

Simon frowned. "I don't know," he admitted. "I guess we'll find out in the morning."

"Morning might be too late!" I countered. "Goblins are nocturnal. Like owls and deer. We should stay up and listen for danger." *Nocturnal* meant that a creature was awake at night and slept during the day.

"Good idea," Simon agreed. "We'll take turns keeping watch. You're first." Then he rolled himself into a blanket and flopped down onto his side with his back to me.

I was shocked. Simon was even braver than I thought if he could sleep at a time like this. "That's it? You're just going to sleep?"

"I'm tired," he mumbled drowsily. "Wake me when you get sleepy."

I stared at him for awhile then finally turned away when I heard him snore softly. With that and the *whisking* of the big knight's whetstone, I couldn't have slept if I'd wanted.

But keeping watch at night is boring, lonely business. Soon my eyes got heavy and started to droop. I couldn't keep them open for another minute....

Hissing voices filled my dreams and I came instantly awake. Someone was right outside our tent. Correction. Some*things* were right outside. Their voices weren't human.

"Jus' a teensie one fer nibblin'?" whined a high-pitched voice. It sounded all sharp and itchy in my ears like fingernails on a chalkboard.

"Not yet, ya dolt," hissed another voice. It was deeper but still not human. "We gots ta find da boss. Den we eats."

Shuffling steps scraped past our tent. "Den we eats 'em all," the deep voice added with a chuckle.

Taking a big gulp to steady myself, I crept toward the tent flap. Even though I had a pretty good idea of what was outside, I still had to make sure.

My heart raced and my breath seemed like it wanted to jump out of my mouth. Normally I don't think I would have been so afraid, but I didn't have a sword and I was outnumbered. I don't think any knight would tease me for being a little nervous just then.

I drew back the tent flap with a shaky hand. Bright moonlight made me blink, but I didn't have any trouble spotting the pair of sneaks. Their pale green skin looked sickly and grey in the light, and their big, round heads bobbed on their skinny necks.

They were goblins, just like I'd suspected. Now all I needed to do was stop them.

Holes in the Hillside

8

When the goblins wandered out of sight, I gently let the tent flap fall back into place. Goblins might not be very smart or strong, but they had terrific hearing.

Next, I scooted over to Simon and nudged him lightly on the shoulder. "Wake up," I called quietly.

"Five more minutes," he mumbled, pulling the blanket over his head.

I might have smiled if two goblins hadn't just walked past the tent talking about eating me. I squatted down and shook Simon. "Get up. There's goblins outside."

He bolted to a sitting position like I'd stuck him with a pin. "Goblins?" he asked bewilderedly. "Where?"

This time I thumped him on the head. "Not in here, peasant. Out there." I pointed at the tent flap. "Two of them."

Simon tugged the blanket up around his shoulders and eyed the flap fearfully. He was awake enough to understand what was happening. "So what do we do?" he asked without taking his eyes from the flap.

"Follow them, I guess," I said with a shrug. I really didn't have any better ideas. "See what they're up to." As a joke, I added, "Stop them from eating anyone."

The scowl Simon shot me said he didn't think my joke was funny.

"We'll just follow them, all right? Don't get excited, peasant."

Simon tossed his blanket at me. "Hey, with the ceremony being cancelled, you're just a peasant, too."

I started to protest but realized I didn't have anything good to say. Simon was right. I really was nothing but a peasant.

And it was all Sir Filabard's fault.

After peeking through the tent flap again for signs of danger, we slipped stealthily outside. The camp was silent except for some snoring coming from a tent here and there. There was no sign of the goblins.

"I saw them this way," I said, then Simon and I scampered to the tents where I'd last seen the goblins. We crouched between the tents and looked out over the campsite.

"I don't know which way they went from here," I told him glumly. I had hoped they wouldn't be out of sight yet.

"Just a sec," Simon said while fishing around in his pockets. He wore a long, sky blue robe dotted with white and silver specks.

It wasn't a very knightly garment and looked more like something a wizard would wear. It had pockets everywhere. Big pockets, little pockets, and secret pockets inside and out.

Simon was always pulling props for his magic tricks out of those pockets. Like apples for juggling. I don't know how such a small kid carried so much weight.

This time he pulled out something oblong and dull white. It was a narrow bone the size of a pencil and tipped with a pointed claw. It might have been a finger bone, but not from a human.

He held the bone up close to his mouth and whispered words to it that I couldn't hear. Then he brushed off a spot on the ground and set the bone in the middle of it.

"This isn't the time for tricks," I scolded sharply. I couldn't believe that he was wasting time on nonsense. We had to find those goblins.

Simon shushed me and held up a finger for silence. He took a deep breath and chanted a little rhyme.

> Finder find
> Where the hidden hides.
> Pointer point,
> Be our guiding guides.

When he finished, he sat back and winked at me.

As we watched the finger bone, it started to move.

Slowly at first, then faster. It wiggled and jerked back and forth in the dirt like a fish on the shore. Its clawed tip whizzed round in a blur.

"What is—?" I started to ask but the bone suddenly stopped moving. Its sharp tip pointed ahead and to our left toward a dark patch of trees on the edge of camp.

Simon scooped up the bone and hid it in one of his many pockets. "That way," he said and pointed to the trees with a nod of his floppy-haired head.

"You can't be serious," I said doubtfully. I didn't believe for a second that a magic trick could tell us where the goblins had gone.

"Ah, ah, ah," Simon replied smugly while shaking a finger at me. "A magician never reveals his secrets." Then he started tiptoeing toward the trees.

They were full of shadowy shapes and bunched up against one side of the valley in a tight cluster. The smell of fresh dirt hung in the air about them like someone had recently dug a deep hole nearby, or maybe a grave.

I grabbed Simon's shoulder. "I'll go first," I told him and he nodded in thanks. He'd been acting brave and very much like a knight, but we both knew which one of us was better in a fight.

Now if I only had my sword, I could prove it.

No matter how careful I tried to be, branches scratched and poked me as I crept through the woods. Every scrape seemed as loud as a shout in the quiet night.

I was starting to have second thoughts. Maybe this wasn't such a good idea.

Goblin ears can hear a mouse twitching its whiskers at one hundred paces. I was afraid they'd hear us coming as surely as if we wore bells around our necks.

A faint, flickering glow ahead told me that we weren't alone. It sputtered like torchlight and we dropped to our hands and knees and inched forward side-by-side when we saw it.

I felt suddenly hot, but it had nothing to do with the temperature. I was afraid. Sweat dampened my skin and I had to clench my jaw to keep my teeth from chattering.

The glow brightened as we approached the wall of the valley. The trees thinned out a bit, too. From their edge, we saw that the light radiated from a cave in the side of the hill.

Simon tapped me on the shoulder and pointed to the left of the cave, then to its right and then above it. The whole side of the hill was pocked with caves. They peppered the hillside like the markings on a spotted dog.

Goblin holes, I realized and suddenly felt light-headed. Whatever the valley was, lots more than two goblins lived there. Probably lots more than two hundred.

"We have to tell someone," I whispered so quietly that even I almost missed hearing it.

But just then the torchlight grew brighter and we collapsed onto our stomachs and held our breath.

Someone was coming!

A man stepped from the cave. Beside him shuffled two goblins. The pair I'd seen earlier.

I was sure of the man's identity, too. By the light of the burning torch in his right hand, I saw the unmistakable sparkle of a jeweled, red ring.

The man was Sir Filabard and he was talking with the pair of goblins like the three of them were old friends!

Removing Rubble

9

Thump. Thump.

The noise was my heart pounding in my chest.

Goblins alone were bad enough, but what was Sir Filabard doing talking and smiling with them? He was supposed to be a knight and the sworn enemy of goblins!

Rebuke All Evil, Act Eighty-four of the *Noble Deeds and Duties* read, *With a Clear Voice and Steady Hand.* It meant that a knight must always stand against evil and never pretend even for a moment to be part of it.

Sir Filabard was breaking all the rules.

"You have cleared away all of the rubble from the tunnel, yes?" he asked the goblins.

The bigger of the two goblins stepped toward Sir Filabard. It wore a grimy eyepatch over its left eye and looked to be a little bit taller than me. Big for a goblin, maybe some kind of leader.

"What about da gold?" it hissed and pointed its claw at

the scruffy knight.

Sir Filabard swatted the goblin's hand away. "Don't threaten me, Schrat. You'll get paid when you complete your task."

"*Champion* Schrat," the big goblin insisted.

Shrugging, Sir Filabard ignored the comment. "The rubble?" he asked again.

"Tomorrow," Schrat rasped. "Den we gets da gold?" He looked hopefully at Sir Filabard.

The scruffy knight smiled broadly. Toying with his ring, he said, "Oh yes, then you will get what is coming to you."

Next to me, Simon gasped. He didn't like the sound of what Sir Filabard had said, and neither did I. It sounded like Sir Filabard didn't plan on paying the goblins their gold.

"Connor," Simon blurted nervously, "we're here to dispose of the goblins for Sir Filabard. He used them for something and now he wants to get rid of them."

His voice was a whisper but I heard him just fine. He'd said exactly what I'd been thinking. Unfortunately, Sir Filabard and the goblins had heard him, too.

Sir Filabard rounded on Schrat. "You were followed?" he demanded.

Schrat cowered from the much taller man. His hands came up defensively over his bald, green head. "N-no," he stammered. "Nobodies followed. Schrat is quiet like death."

That seemed to calm Sir Filabard a bit, but he still stared

suspiciously in our direction.

"Go out and look," he ordered. "I cannot permit witnesses to live."

Simon whimpered softly and I squeezed my eyes shut in disbelief, trying to clear my thoughts. Had Sir Filabard just said that he'd kill us for spying on him? Being friendly with goblins was one thing, but threatening to kill fellow knights was unthinkable.

Goblin Champion Schrat and his smaller companion shuffled toward the woods and our hiding spot. They'd trip over us if we didn't move.

"Quick," I hissed into Simon's ear, "the caves!"

I shot up and dragged Simon to his feet. With a hard shove to his back, I got him running then followed right on his heels.

"Kill them!" Sir Filabard shouted before we'd taken two steps. The goblins hooted and hissed in response.

I glanced at the caves and then over my shoulder. The goblins were coming in fast. Their grinning, toothy faces bobbed from side to side as they thumped after us on their big, flat feet.

We ran, but the caves were too far off. We weren't going to make it.

Magic Tricks

10

I sprinted harder than I ever had. Ahead of me, Simon zipped into one of the caves and disappeared.

The goblins panted heavily behind me, and hot breath beat against my neck. Something swiped at the back of my doublet but didn't catch hold.

Screaming, I darted through the mouth of the cave straight into…

Nothingness.

Darkness crowded all about me like I'd jumped into a lake of black. The moonlight, Sir Filabard's torch, the stars—they all vanished.

I stopped and spun around, holding my breath. I couldn't see or hear anything. Not the goblins. Not Simon.

I tried to scream but managed only a long, silent exhale.

What was this place? Where had everyone gone?

Then a hand grabbed the front of my doublet and pulled me roughly ahead, almost knocking me over.

"Hurry," Simon's voice hissed from the blackness, "the spell of darkness won't last long." I couldn't see him at all. I couldn't even see my own hands.

We ran again. I don't know for how long or how far. In the darkness, time and distance didn't matter. There was only nothingness. If not for Simon's hand, I could have been floating through space.

Suddenly blue light sparked to life, stinging my eyes. When I could see again, Simon stood in front of me holding a glowing blue sphere. I would have called it a ball except it looked completely made of light.

"What was that?" I asked about the nothingness. "Where are we? What are you holding?" I had so many questions.

Simon slumped weakly against the rough stone wall of the cave. That's when I noticed how white his face looked and that he was sweating. He slid to the floor with a soft thud.

"Magician's secrets," he wheezed. He looked exhausted.

I squatted down in front of him. "Are you going to be all right? Did the goblins…?" I couldn't understand why he was so tired. We hadn't run *that* far.

"No, no. The goblins didn't do anything," he breathed quietly. "I just need to rest."

I squinted at him, still confused. I was missing something.

He rolled his eyes at me and forced a little smile. "Magic, you peasant," he said. "Casting magic makes me tired."

That made me grin. He must really be tired if he expected me to believe him. Magic, my eye! "You've been reading too many books," I teased.

Simon frowned. "You can't be…" he started, then raised the glowing sphere level with his mouth. He puffed out a breath and the sphere gently glided away from his palm.

It floated straight at me.

"Take it, if you can," he smirked.

I reached out my hand to take the sphere, but it passed right through. I tried again with the same result. No matter how hard I tried I couldn't grab the sphere.

"What gives?" I asked.

Simon stood slowly and plucked the sphere out of the air as easily as he'd pick a ball off the floor. "Magic," he told me. "My magic, so it won't let you touch it."

My mouth fell open. Was Simon really a wizard, not just a kid who liked magic tricks?

I had more questions than when we'd come out of the black nothingness.

A Cramped Crevice

11

Questions and more questions. I had bunches of them, but one nagged me most of all.

Was Simon a real wizard?

I'd never considered it before. It had never even crossed my mind. Sure, Simon could do magic tricks and juggle, but real magic was different.

"We'd better get going," Simon said before I could pin down all my questions about his secret. "The goblins will catch us soon."

Still shocked, I nodded mutely as Simon struggled to his feet. Together we started down the rocky passageway. Simon's blue sphere didn't seem quite as bright, and that gave me a bad feeling.

As we trekked farther into the cave, the passageway narrowed until we had to walk in single file. Large rocks cluttered our path and the floor rose and fell unevenly. Every step was dangerous. Only by carefully watching our feet did we avoid twisting an ankle or worse.

Eventually the tunnel narrowed to just a jagged crevice between two boulders sticking out from the walls and we stopped. It looked like a dead end.

I pushed against one of the boulders in frustration. It didn't budge. "Now what do we do?" I wondered aloud.

"Here, stand back," Simon requested and stepped right up to the crevice. He held the glowing sphere up to his lips and exhaled loudly.

Rolling slowly, the blue sphere glided into the crevice and disappeared. Darkness crowded around us and I suddenly wondered about what kept all the rock above us from falling down on our heads.

Simon poked his head into the crevice. "It looks like a cavern on the other side," he said, his voice muffled by the boulders. "I think I can see something metal. Tools maybe...."

Simon pulled his head out and turned sharply to me. "I'm going in," he told me determinedly.

"That's not..." I started to reply but then quickly thought about our options. We could either squeeze through the crevice or stand around and wait for the goblins to catch us.

The words to Act Fifty-seven of the *Noble Deeds and Duties* popped into my head:

Beware Danger, Not the Unknown.

That meant there was no point in letting your imagination scare you.

We wouldn't know what was on the other side of the crevice until we investigated. But as for the goblins behind us, they were something to worry about.

I grabbed Simon's arm and tugged him away from the crevice. "Wiggling through caves is a knight's job," I told him firmly. "Wizards go second."

If real danger did lurk on the other side of the crevice, I knew Simon was too tired to handle it. I *had* to go first.

I exhaled for as long as I could then squeezed sideways into the crevice. At first I didn't have any trouble squirming my way through. I kept my eyes closed and thought about the cavern Simon had seen on the other side.

Halfway through, I got stuck.

My eyes popped open but saw nothing but darkness. It was like being in Simon's black spell again, only I couldn't move.

Sharp edges along the boulders dug into my back and chest. Dirt rained down from somewhere above to trickle along my face and neck, itching like a spider slinking across my skin.

In that instant, stuck, I forgot all about being a knight. I forgot about bravery, being a hero, and the *Noble Deeds and Duties*.

So I did the logical thing.

I screamed.

My whole body tightened and I howled from all the way down in my boots. I screamed at being stuck, about the Turning of the Pages being cancelled, and at Sir Filabard for stealing my horse.

And a miraculous thing happened. I found the strength to squirm the rest of the way through the crevice.

Rocks tore at my clothing and skin, and more dirt poured onto my head, but I made it. I shot suddenly out of the crevice and tumbled weakly to the ground in a large cavern. Simon's glowing sphere blinked faintly near the ceiling.

Simon slipped through the crevice behind me without any trouble. Being small, I realized, has advantages.

Together we looked about the roomy cavern. It was oval-shaped with the far ends hidden in shadow. Straight ahead of us, a short, rounded tunnel led into darkness. A wood and metal track disappeared into the tunnel and two rusty mining carts sat motionless on the track.

Other than those and a jumble of battered tools leaning against a wall, the room was empty. We'd reached a dead end.

"Dere's light inside, boss," a muffled voice came from the other side of the crevice.

Simon and I both gasped. We recognized the stuffy-nosed accent right away.

The goblins had caught us and were about to enter the crevice.

Lance and Lever

12

A scuffling noise came from the crevice followed by an angry goblin's voice. "Da champion goes first, runt. Outta da way."

More noise and scratching sounds reached our ears.

"Hurry, we've got to do something!" I shouted, but Simon didn't seem to hear me. He was staring up at the blue sphere with his arms in the air. His lips moved but I couldn't hear what he was saying.

I dashed to the pile of tools. There were a few shovels, some chisels, a pickaxe, and a cracked wooden beam. Mining equipment, not weapons.

An idea struck me and I hefted the cracked beam into my arms. It was heavy and awkward to carry but I managed to level it straight out in front of me like a lance.

"For honor!" I bellowed and charged toward the crevice. I'm not sure where the words came from but they seemed like the right thing to say at the time.

A pale green goblin arm appeared from the crevice. Long dirty fingernails scraped against the rock.

Goblin Champion Schrat's over-sized head appeared next. Seeing me racing forward, he widened his one eye in alarm and hissed at me, frantically scrambling back into the crevice.

My lance crashed into the crevice, scraping and clacking loudly against the rocky walls. The impact stung my hands and sent a hot tingling sensation into my arms. Tiny bits of rubble tumbled from the ceiling, and a cloud of dust welled up from the crevice like steam from a boiling kettle.

Schrat yelped from inside the crevice just as the wooden beam slipped from my grasp and became lodged between the boulders. Dust continued to swirl about the opening and I couldn't see anything inside.

I thudded heavily into one boulder, coughing on dust. From just that little bit of exercise, I was sweating.

"Connor, come on!" Simon urged. I spun around to see him sitting in one of the rusty mine carts. He waved his arms wildly at me to hurry.

I gave the beam a final shove to keep it in place, then ran to the carts.

"The lever," said Simon, pointing to my left. "Pull it and jump in."

The lever stuck up from one side of the metal tracks. It had a leather handgrip and a dark grease stain. It wasn't pointing straight up but more at an angle toward the crevice across the room.

I gave it a tug but it didn't budge.

"It's stuck," I complained. I pulled again but the lever still wouldn't move.

Maybe I just wasn't strong enough.

A loud clatter came from the crevice and I glanced up to see the wooden beam crash to the floor. The goblins would be through any second.

Behind me, Simon chanted loudly:

> Soap, butter, oil, and grease—
> Soak lever, slip release.

When he stopped chanting, he yelled "Now!"

Concentrating and using all my strength, I hauled on the lever. This time it slid back so easily that I tripped onto my backside. It was like playing tug-of-war when the other team surprises you by letting go of the rope.

There was a loud *click* from the tracks followed by the sound of movement like a ball rolling across a floor.

"Connor!" Simon hollered as I scrambled to my feet.

The cart he was sitting in started to roll smoothly along the track toward the tunnel in the wall. I jumped toward it and threw out my hands to catch it, but I was too slow.

My fingers slapped painfully against the side of the cart and I landed on the tracks with a thud.

From my stomach, I watched Simon wheel through the

mouth of the tunnel and vanish down into darkness.

I was alone again, and the goblins were right behind me.

Dark Ride

13

"Dere you is!" shouted Schrat, the goblin champion, triumphantly. He gave a vicious laugh.

I scrambled onto my hands and knees and spun to face the goblin. Crouching and ready for action, I quickly scanned the area.

Schrat stood on the other side of the cavern. He had a toothy smirk on his green face and a curved sword in one hand. He held a smoky torch in the other hand. For some reason, he wasn't coming toward me.

Scraping sounds came from the crevice and I realized that Schrat was waiting for help.

The remaining mine cart was just to my right. If I could climb inside and get it moving down the tracks, Schrat wouldn't be able to follow me.

Schrat noticed me looking at the cart and took a small step forward. "Don' try nuttin' stupid, human," he warned me and waved his sword threateningly.

Goblins are known for two things. Eating, which I've mentioned, and being cowards.

That told me Schrat probably wouldn't attack until his friend showed up. But by the noise coming from the crevice, that wouldn't be long. I had to do something now.

My eyes met Schrat's one-eyed stare and he hissed menacingly. I stared back so hard that he didn't notice me pick up an apple-sized rock.

In one motion, I leapt to my feet, hurled the rock, and jumped into the mine cart. I didn't realize it until I stopped, but I was screaming the whole time.

Just as the rock smacked into the side of Schrat's bloated head, I crashed headfirst into the cart. My weight started it rolling slowly down the tracks.

Schrat howled in pain. I doubted that the rock had injured him, but it had surprised him. A goblin's head is too thick to be hurt by a rock.

I sat up in time to see Schrat coming at me with his curved sword held high. His eyepatch had been knocked aside by the rock to reveal a perfectly good second eye. He didn't need the eyepatch at all!

Why would he wear an eyepatch he doesn't need? I wondered just as he sliced his sword at my head. I ducked in time to feel the wind from his attack *whoosh* right over me.

Any closer and I'd have been a whole lot shorter.

Lucky for me, Schrat didn't have time for another attack.

The cart rapidly gained speed and whisked me into the tunnel. The goblin and the light from his torch quickly disappeared.

I was alone, deep underground, and in the dark. I screamed for a long time.

The cart zipped along the tracks, racing deeper down and down. It zoomed around curves, down sharp drops, and over bumpy patches I feared might bounce me out of the cart.

It certainly hadn't been designed with riders in mind.

The ride went on for what seemed like forever. Wind howled in my ears and dark rock walls flew past.

The whole time, I laid on my back repeating the words to Act Ninety-one of the *Noble Deeds and Duties*:

A Single Light Pierces the Darkness.

I'm not really sure what the words meant, but they seemed to fit right then.

Finally, the cart slowed as the track gradually leveled off. Ahead I saw a faint blue glow.

Simon's sphere! I thought hopefully and sat up.

Squinting, I watched shapes materialize like ghosts out of the darkness. The tunnel walls around me, rocks here and there, finally Simon's cart. It was parked at the end of the tracks in front of a rounded stone wall.

My cart bumped into Simon's and I eagerly clambered

out. "Simon!" I called again and again, tripping on the edge of my cart in excitement and crawling over the rocky ground.

The blue light came from Simon's cart, but he didn't answer me.

Nervously, I peeked inside. Near the bottom, the blue sphere twinkled up at me.

As I watched, it blinked once then faded into nothingness. I was alone and in the dark again.

And Simon was missing.

14

My chest tightened and I slumped wearily to the hard ground.

Where could Simon be?

I had no light, no map, and no idea where I was.

I don't think I've ever felt as small and helpless as I did then. Not even when Sir Filabard had stolen Honormark.

A loud grinding rumbled to my left but I couldn't see anything in the dark. The noise echoed loudly throughout the cavern like a growl and I thought the roof might collapse.

A sliver of reddish light appeared along the ground near the rounded stone wall. As I watched, it grew brighter and I saw a section of the wall swing open.

It was a door! A secret door made to look exactly like the rest of the wall.

Someone stepped through the door.

"Connor?"

It was Simon. His shaggy red hair was a mess but he looked fine other than that. He held a burning torch in one hand.

"Simon!" I exclaimed. "Where did you go?"

He pointed excitedly at something behind him. "There's a stairway here," he said hurriedly. "I think it must lead somewhere important."

"Like where important?" I nodded at him but couldn't guess what he was trying to tell me.

Simon frowned in thought for a moment. "I'm not sure," he admitted, "but do you remember Sir Filabard asking the goblins about rubble?"

This time when I nodded, I didn't say a thing. I remembered Sir Filabard asking, but I couldn't see what it had to do with a hidden stairway. Rubble was usually a pile of rocks in someone's way....

Suddenly I felt a little dense.

"Sir Filabard is looking for something," Simon continued, "and I bet you it's down those stairs."

Everything made sense then. Why we were here and why Sir Filabard was friendly with goblins.

The tunnel had been filled with rubble and Sir Filabard had hired the goblins to dig it out. He wanted whatever was down those stairs but couldn't get to it without the goblins' help.

"What do you think it is?" I asked. I meant the thing Filabard was looking for.

"Gold probably," he shrugged, "or some lost treasure."

I stood up and brushed myself off. "We've got to find out, you know," I said seriously.

Simon nodded. "I know, I know. *Duty Calls At Any Hour*," he quoted Act Seventy-nine.

"Exactly," I agreed with a smile and took the torch from him. As knights-to-be, it was our responsibility to investigate.

Besides, we couldn't exactly get out of the tunnel with the goblins behind us. Exploring was really our only option.

I paused before stepping through the stone door. "Who knows," I grinned excitedly, "it might be fun."

I know I liked the idea of exploring a lot more than I liked running from goblins and a scruffy-looking knight.

Simon didn't look so sure. His face was a little pale.

Taking a deep breath, I started down the stairs.

Castle Burrowfar

15

The stairs descended in a tight spiral down a narrow passage. After just a few steps, we couldn't see how far we had come or how far we still had to go.

Grey-white cobwebs blanketed the passage in thick strands and patches like nets. They sizzled and sparked in the fire of my torch. Dust covered the floor and our footsteps echoed hollowly all about.

I counted one hundred steps, then two hundred, and more before we reached the bottom.

The stairway ended at a large steel door etched with strange sigils. A *sigil* is a magical symbol.

Simon blew on the door to clear away the dust and squinted at the etchings.

"Burrowfar," he said finally. "That's the name of this place. But I can't make out anything else. The symbols aren't familiar."

Careful not to touch any of the sigils, I pushed against the door. It felt oddly warm and alive. Creaking slowly open, rust flaked from its hinges.

A cool breeze brushed against our faces from a long, wide hallway beyond. Faded paintings covered the walls and small doors of different shapes led to places unknown.

A set of crystal double doors stood closed at the far end of the hallway.

"What is this place?" I whispered, hesitant to speak loudly.

"I think it's a castle," Simon answered softly. "We came in through a tower and now we're in the main area. The inner bailey, I think it's called."

Most castles have an *inner* and *outer bailey*. They're the areas inside the protective walls. The space between the outside walls is the outer bailey and the space inside that is the inner bailey.

But if this place was a castle, how did it get here? I'd never heard of a castle being built underground.

"Let's try those doors at the end of the hall," I suggested.

Walking close together, we crept along the hall. The paintings on the walls were faded and covered with dust. We couldn't quite figure out what they were supposed to be, but they were full of different colors.

The doors swung open silently by themselves when we reached the end of the hall. It was like the doors had known we were coming.

"Magic," Simon said with a brief nod. "Whoever lived

here used magic."

I didn't reply but stared into the huge room beyond with my torch held high. The room was too big for the torch to light completely. Shadows darkened the corners and ceiling.

Wide stone pillars ran in two rows down the middle of the room. They ended before a short flight of stairs that led to a low, flat platform.

Ten crystal thrones sat on the raised platform. They looked like they'd been built with children in mind.

We inched forward cautiously.

"*Mcaw!*"

A piercing cry erupted in the quiet of the great room.

We glanced up just in time to see a small dark blur speeding toward us from above. Blazing yellow eyes filled with hate stared back at us.

"Look out!" I roared and shoved Simon to the floor. Instantly, I threw myself down next to him.

"*Mcaw!*" came the cry again.

A flutter of wings passed over our heads and brought a choking stench of death and decay to our nostrils.

Gagging, I rolled onto my back and raised my arms to ward off an attack. But one never came. The dark shape zipped out the double doors and was gone.

Simon and I didn't move for several minutes. We panted breathlessly on the cold stone floor waiting for our hearts to fall down out of our throats.

Finally, Simon asked, "Was that a raven?"

I forced my dry throat to swallow before responding. "I think so, but something was wrong with it. It smelled—"

"Dead," Simon finished my thought for me.

"Yeah, dead. Like it was rotten and half decayed," I added.

Simon rolled onto his side to look at me seriously. "We have to be careful," he warned. "There's a kind of wizard that can command the dead. They're called *necromancers*. They're very evil."

I closed my eyes. *Necromancers? The living dead? What had we gotten ourselves into?*

Suddenly, Act Sixteen came to my mind:

Doubt Not the Strength of Righteousness.

In other words, we couldn't give up. We might be up against Sir Filabard, necromancers, goblins, and the living dead, but we had to go on.

I was determined to solve the mystery of this castle, and I knew Simon felt the same. We climbed to our feet and approached the thrones again.

"We should make a plan," Simon advised.

I agreed. Stumbling blindly around the castle wasn't going to get us anywhere but lost.

"Weapons," I said. "We need weapons to protect ourselves." I was thinking of the raven. We'd been lucky it was only a bird.

"Where are we going to find weapons?" Simon asked doubtfully. "We don't know where anything is."

"The armory. Every...." I started to say *Every castle has an armory* but never got the chance to finish. An *armory* is where a castle's guards keep their weapons.

When I said *armory*, a throne behind me came to life. It leapt into the air and smacked me in the knees, knocking me into its seat.

Strange wooden tentacles wiggled out from its dusty cushions like snakes to wrap around my chest and over my thighs. They sprouted from the armrests, too, and coiled about my wrists.

"Simon, what's happening?" I cried in alarm.

The tentacles held me prisoner in the throne. I feared they would choke me or burrow into my skin.

Then the whole throne jerked suddenly and lurched forward, scooting through the air. Simon jumped, trying to catch me, but the throne was too high.

"Simon!" I screamed as the throne turned and began to soar toward the doors. The sensation of flying tickled my stomach uncomfortably.

Before I could scream again, I rocketed through the doors and down the hallway we'd been in earlier.

The throne was taking me somewhere, but where?

Knight Scares

16

The throne whizzed down the hallway. Paintings and doors flew past in a blur of colors. Ahead, the steel door covered with sigils waited like the ground waits for someone to fall.

I closed my eyes and screamed. A knight shouldn't die sitting down, even in a flying throne.

At the last second, the throne twisted sharply and sped left. My eyes popped open in astonishment.

A small green door had opened and we raced through it into a second long passage.

Maybe the throne wasn't trying to kill me. Maybe it was taking me somewhere terrible.

Images of torture chambers and dark dungeon cells filled my mind as we continued to zoom through the castle.

When the throne finally stopped flying and dropped gently to the floor, I realized how wrong I'd been. The throne's tentacles slithered off me and disappeared into the cushions and armrests.

I was in the castle's armory and everything suddenly made sense.

Earlier I'd mentioned wanting a weapon. When I'd said the word *armory*, the throne had reacted. Somehow, it had understood what I'd said.

Simon had been right in calling this a magical castle.

The armory held more weapons than I'd ever seen before. Crossed swords and daggers lined the walls. Pikes and halberds rested in carved wooden stands. Bows and slings hung on special racks from the ceiling. Weapons were everywhere and there were enough of them to supply an army.

Anything I could have wanted was there, and they were even a bit on the small side. Like the thrones, the weapons seemed made for children.

Even with all the choices, it didn't take me long to find the perfect sword. A silver-edged, black steel falchion.

A *falchion* is a short sword with a thick blade that narrows toward the tip. It's short and light enough for someone my age to use. I might be big, but I was still a kid.

The falchion was in the hands of a dusty suit of kid-sized plate armor standing in a corner. It took me a bit of work to pry open its rusty grip and free the sword, and I immediately wished I hadn't done it.

Ffffft-thunk!

A crossbow bolt zipped by my head and buried itself deep

in a wooden weapon rack. A *bolt* is a special type of arrow used in a crossbow.

I looked up to see a cluster of little armored knights coming toward me from across the room. The knights were just empty suits of armor but they were moving and acting exactly like soldiers.

Five of them clunked heavily forward with loaded crossbows in their hands.

Snick-thwang! went their crossbows and five bolts screamed straight at me.

With a shout, I dove to the floor and rolled behind the nearest weapon rack. Bolts clacked off the stone walls above my head. Others *thunked* into the wooden rack.

If I hadn't heard the first shot, I'd be dead.

Lucky for me, the armor-knights were slow and clumsy. After firing their crossbows, they dropped them and stiffly marched ahead. They took up weapons from stands and racks as they advanced.

If I was quick, I might be able to dash around the knights and escape through the door.

Clutching my new sword in both hands, I waited tensely for them to come nearer. Like I'd hoped, the five of them headed around the same side of the weapon rack.

The side to my right was clear. I had a straight shot to the door.

The first knight rounded on me with a spiked mace held high, and I threw up my falchion to block the attack.

Sparks exploded from the metallic clash, but I held my ground and pushed. The knight clumsily fell back into its companions with a hollow *thwong* and I ran.

Simon burst through the door at the same time on a second flying throne.

"Connor, grab on!" he shouted urgently.

He'd noticed what I hadn't. Dozens of armored knights were coming alive all about the armory. Their rusty joints screeched deafeningly. Each of them had a weapon and was coming straight at me.

I jumped for Simon's throne and managed to grab a rung along the bottom with one hand.

Simon didn't wait for me to get a better grip. "Treasury!" he commanded the throne.

In response, the throne spun around and flew back out the door, dragging me with it.

The Birdcage

17

With my feet bouncing and scraping on the floor, we sped along twisting passages, steep stairways, and great halls with high arched ceilings.

My hand and arm ached and my feet throbbed, but I couldn't let go. The throne was moving too quickly. I'd never be able to keep up on foot.

From above, Simon shouted encouragingly all the way. "Hang on, Connor!" and "Almost there!" he called.

I grunted in response. How did he know we were almost there? I know he was trying to help, but it was a silly thing to say.

Peasant, I thought grumpily.

At last we passed through a round yellow door between two small human-like statues and the throne floated to the floor. I let go and rolled out of its way then tiredly pushed myself to my feet.

I had my sword and it was a fine, handsome blade, but

had it been worth getting? I was so tired and sore that I doubted I could use it.

Climbing excitedly out of the throne, Simon gasped. "Connor—look," he exclaimed.

Sparkling treasure twinkled everywhere.

Gold coins spilled out of chests. Jewelry dangled from silver statues. Gems sparkled from display cases and peeked from polished cups and bowls like pieces of fruit.

I'd never imagined so much treasure in one place.

"This is what Sir Filabard is after," Simon whispered without taking his eyes from the twinkling hoard.

"He'd be the richest man in the kingdom," I agreed. "In five kingdoms."

I couldn't get over the amount of treasure. There was enough to make every person in Tiller's Field rich.

But Sir Filabard wanted it all for himself, and that was wrong. Knights weren't supposed to be greedy:

Wealth Cannot Tip the Scale of Character

read Act Thirty-five, and it meant that honor and kindness made a good knight, not riches or treasure.

"We can't let him get it," I said. Sir Filabard was a bad man. There's no telling what kind of trouble he'd cause with so much gold.

About to respond, Simon turned to me just as a soft voice echoed from the far side of the heaping mound of treasure.

"H-hello*...lo*?" it beckoned weakly.

Simon and I froze. We'd both been sure the castle was deserted of other people.

I gripped my black falchion tightly and swallowed. "Who's there?" I demanded.

The voice coughed dryly. "Please help*...elp* me," it pleaded. It sounded like a breeze rustling dead leaves.

I shook my head. "Show yourself first."

Suddenly there was a great flutter of wings and the stink of death we'd smelled earlier. Coughing, we covered our mouths and noses against the awful stench.

From the opposite side of the room rose a shadowy mass of wings, beaks, and burning yellow eyes. It was a small flock of ravens, maybe ten of them.

Bunched closely together, they glided toward us like a dark cloud. They clutched something metal in their sharp talons.

It was a birdcage. Rounded at the top, it was made of thin iron bars that curved down to a flat base. The cage was battered and many of its bars bent or broken.

Inside the cage was a dingy grey skull with a long silver beard. The beard dangled out of the cage and the skull had a strange blood red marking on one side.

The sound of rustling leaves came again. "Help me*...e* please," the skull begged.

Terror in the Tower

18

"What—who are you?" Simon gasped hoarsely from behind the hand he held over his nose and mouth.

I nodded to him, unable to speak. The stench of the ravens was horrible. It made my eyes sting and water.

The skull did not respond, but the ravens glided closer. If their stink hadn't told me something, a closer look did.

The ravens were dead. What little was left of their feathers was wilted or decaying. Dingy white bone peeked through missing patches of skin.

"My children...*ren*," the skull whispered without opening its jaw. I don't know how it spoke without vocal cords, but its breezy voice echoed dreamily.

Simon and I dropped to our knees and bowed our heads. "Yes, master," we said at the same time.

The skull chuckled dryly and goose pimples popped up along my arms.

Something wasn't right. I felt strangely warm and tired

like I'd just eaten a big holiday meal.

"I am Lord Nebbezim," the skull declared and its whisper shouted inside my head. "We are friends...*ends*, and you must help me to escape...*ape*."

Simon and I nodded agreeably. Of course we'd help. Knights helped those in need, especially their friends. And we were friends with the skull. It had said so.

Something didn't feel quite right, but I nodded and grinned stupidly at Lord Nebbezim anyway. I couldn't help myself. He was such a nice talking skull!

With a fluttering of wings, the ravens lowered the bird-cage to the floor. "One of you pick me up," Nebbezim ordered. "We must leave immediately...*ately*"

Simon and I rushed forward. We reached the cage at the same time and began pushing each other for the privilege to carry it.

I wanted so much to please Lord Nebbezim. He was my friend.

With my feet planted, I shoved Simon solidly in the chest. He stumbled over a shiny treasure box then slipped as gold coins spilled and clattered onto the stone floor.

Ha! Serves you right, I thought victoriously and scooped up the cage. *You can have the gold, silly Simon. I get to carry Lord Nebbezim.*

"Enough play," Nebbezim warned. "Simon, take a torch and lead us out. It is a long walk to my tower...*wer*. You and Connor will require light...*ight*."

Funny, I didn't remember telling Lord Nebbezim our names.

Simon bounded eagerly to his feet. He scowled briefly at me after he'd taken a torch from the wall then headed out of the treasury.

I followed with a smug smile on my face. I had won our little contest. I was sure that I was Lord Nebbezim's favorite.

Under Lord Nebbezim's direction, we followed a confusing path through the quiet castle. Behind us we occasionally heard the faint rustle of wings but nothing else. The castle was as dead as the ravens.

"Where are we going, master?" I asked after we'd been marching for at least half an hour.

In the back of my mind, I knew that calling the skull *master* was wrong, but the word just popped out of my mouth the way *father* and *mother* do when I'm talking to my parents.

"My tower," Nebbezim snapped. "I told you that...*at*. Now no more questions. I must prepare myself for rebirth...*irth*."

Rebirth? I wondered. I didn't have any idea what that meant, but I trusted Lord Nebbezim. If something was important for me to know, he'd tell me.

At last we stood before a wide wooden door with a rounded top. More symbols decorated the door, but if Simon could read any of them this time, he didn't let me know.

The hallway before the door was full of short statues of men and women in battle poses. They held weapons and shields and looked incredibly life-like. None of them was much taller than me.

"Now open...*pen* the door to my tower," Nebbezim hissed.

We jumped to obey, and it took both of us to push it open. As it creaked open, a stomach-churning scent of death gusted from the tower like a belch in our faces.

We choked on the stench and Lord Nebbezim laughed. "Be alert now, my children...*ren*. The tower is cursed with the undead."

Simon and I both frowned. Lord Nebbezim was talking in riddles and we wanted so very much to help him. Curses? The undead? There was so much to know about our new friend!

We entered huddling tightly together. I gripped Nebbezim's birdcage in my left hand and my falchion in my right. Simon held the torch above his head.

Inside, the horrible stink was almost too much for us. Simon pulled the collar of his robes up over his face, but all I could do was hold my breath because my hands were full.

The door led to a wide, circular room with tall book-shelves lining the walls. Short tables cluttered with books, papers, and scrolls stood between pairs of heavy chairs. A curved staircase climbed up to the tower's second level.

It was the chairs that caught my attention. Or to be exact, what was in them.

Skeletons. Maybe twenty of them.

Some wore battered metal breastplates or dented helms, but all of them were armed. They carried swords, spears, and battle hammers.

All at once, the skeletons turned their yellowed skulls to us and their crooked jaws dropped open with a great *clack*. Cold green flame burned in their empty eye sockets.

Creaking and clattering, the skeletons raised their weapons and stood.

Rebirth

19

"To the stairs...*airs*, children. Be quick!" Nebbezim's echo sounded urgent, but we really didn't need to be told to run. The skeletons were approaching.

Fortunately they weren't very fast. They moved stiffly with their feet scratching heavily across the stones of the floor like they'd just awakened.

A lone skeleton blocked our path to the stairs. It wore a huge helm with curving horns and held a rusty spear in both hands.

I didn't pause when I saw it. Lord Nebbezim needed me to hurry.

Leading with my shoulder and shouting wildly, I charged into the skeleton before it could react. Smacking into its bony body was like running into a tree. Its arms and ribcage slapped against me like branches.

Smack! Thump! Snap!

My shoulder took the skeleton square in the chest and we

crashed to the floor. Its frail bones fell apart and snapped beneath me like twigs.

The battle had been almost too easy!

I rolled instantly to my knees and clawed to get free. I'd never felt more like a knight! Finger bones clung to my clothing, but I hadn't taken the worst of it.

The skeleton was in pieces. Its scattered bones twitched with undead life, but they were spread out in a broken wreck. The skeleton wasn't going to get up anytime soon.

Ahead of me, Simon sprinted up the stairs. He carried Lord Nebbezim's birdcage and I realized I must have dropped it in the collision. My falchion was missing, too.

An icy hand gripped my shoulder and I snatched the first thing I could find. It was a leg bone—the *femur*. It's part of the leg that makes up the thigh.

Twisting around hard, I swung my bone-club at the skeleton behind me.

Clack-crack! I connected with the skeleton's knees and the undead monster toppled to its side. It awkwardly swiped at me with its short sword but missed by a long shot.

Again I felt like a valiant knight. I had single-handedly defeated two enemies!

At least that's how I felt until I looked up to see a swarm of skeletons marching toward me. From there, it didn't take me long to decide that even the bravest knight knows when he's outnumbered.

I might have handled two skeletons, but eighteen were

too many.

I hopped to my feet and ran. Behind me, the scratching of bony feet followed. Ahead, Simon and Lord Nebbezim had vanished.

I started taking the stairs two at a time but quickly tired. I'd used up so much energy already. After rounding the first bend, I slowed down.

For a while at least, I'd outrun the skeletons.

The stairs continued up without an end in sight. Faint light glowed from somewhere above, but I couldn't tell if it was from Simon's torch or something else.

I leaned heavily against the wall and closed my eyes. Everything was happening so fast and I couldn't catch my breath. First Sir Filabard and his goblins. Now Lord Nebbezim and the skeletons....

What are we doing here? I suddenly wondered. *Why are we taking orders from a talking skull?*

Then I remembered Simon mentioning evil wizards who commanded the dead. He'd called them necromancers. Nebbezim must be one of them.

My stomach cramped painfully and I shivered with a chilling spasm. The warm sleepiness I'd felt when Nebbezim spoke was gone. It was replaced by a feeling of horror and disgust.

But what is he planning? I asked myself. *What could an undead skull want?*

One word flashed in my head. *Rebirth.* It echoed like

one of Nebbezim's eerie whispers.

Nebbezim had said that he was preparing for rebirth.

I thought about that. The prefix *re* meant *again* and *birth* meant *to be born*. Putting them together, I decided, meant *to be born again*.

Suddenly I understood Nebbezim's plan. He'd been turned into a skull and trapped in the birdcage. To escape, he needed something in the tower…something that would free him.

My head shot up and I gasped in horror. Simon and I had been helping a necromancer.

How could we have let that happen?

From above, Simon's voice called down the winding stairway. "Hurry, Connor, our master needs help."

I sneered in disgust. I was ashamed to have called Nebbezim *master*. The idea was sickening.

But I knew what I had to do now. I was finally thinking straight again.

"Coming," I called up the stairs in my best fake, sleepy voice. Then I added "master".

I tightened my grip on the leg bone and started back up the stairs.

Skeletons on the Stairs

20

I found Simon at the top of the stairs on a long landing. A stout iron-bound door prevented him from going any farther. He cradled Nebbezim's cage close to his chest with one hand and pushed against the door with the other.

His torch burned from a sconce on the wall. A *sconce* is like a candle holder only larger and for torches.

I cleared my throat and Simon turned around with a start. "It's stuck," he explained. "Give me a hand."

I didn't move to help him. Instead, I brought up my bone club threateningly. "Give me the birdcage," I demanded.

Simon stared at me and smirked. "I'm carrying Lord Nebbezim now. You had your chance."

Simon didn't understand. He was still confused by the skull's hypnotic spell. He thought I wanted the cage out of jealousy.

I was going to have to take it by force.

I dropped into a fighting stance and took a step closer.

Simon wasn't a match for me, but he used magic. I had to be cautious.

He fumbled hurriedly in the pockets of his robes for something to help him cast a spell. I couldn't let him find it.

With my weapon raised, I charged. Simon was my friend and I hated what I had to do, but I couldn't think of anything else. The skeletons were still behind us and I didn't have much time before they arrived.

My only hope was to get the cage before either of us got hurt.

With a mighty swing, I sliced at the birdcage but never finished my attack. As I brought my arm down, it suddenly felt heavy and slow like it was moving underwater.

"Come to me, my child...*ild*," Nebbezim whispered soothingly, and a feeling of calm seeped through my body. The femur slipped from my fingers and rolled noisily down the stairs.

I couldn't move!

My eyes darted back and forth between the birdcage and my fallen weapon as it tumbled away. I was powerless to do anything else.

"Assist us, Connor...*nor*," Nebbezim ordered. "We are close now. Your master...*ter* must live again."

A familiar, warm drowsiness clouded my mind and I forgot what I'd been thinking. New thoughts whispered to me like bits of half-remembered dreams.

It would be so easy to help Simon open the door. That's

all Lord Nebbezim wanted. Would it be such a bad thing to do?

Numbly I reached for the door's handle. Everything would be better once we opened the door. We just had to hurry.

Whoomp!

A battle hammer crashed solidly into the door just as my fingers grasped the handle. Splinters and a cloud of dust exploded into the air.

We wheeled about to see the troop of skeletons climbing the stairs. Their limbs creaked and groaned as they ascended.

Now we didn't have any choice. We had to get the door opened or we'd be trapped.

"Push, Simon!" I shouted and threw myself against the door. He slammed himself next to me and heaved with his shoulder.

Creaking, the door budged slightly. We pushed again, but cold fingers snatched my collar and spun me around before I could sneak through.

Skeletons crowded before me at the foot of the landing like a living wall of bone. Their cruel green eyes stared hard into mine. Their weapons screamed at my head.

I dropped to the floor with a grunt as the wind from their attack whistled over my head. I landed with my arms outstretched.

That was all it took. The shock, the speed, the jolt on the

floor. Something snapped in my mind. My thoughts cleared and I was me again. Connor, knight-to-be. Connor, enemy of necromancers everywhere.

I rolled as the front line of skeletons attacked again. This time their rusty weapons clanged on the floor. Sparks flared where they struck.

Leaping to my feet, I turned to the door before the skeletons could attack again. Simon had squirmed through the narrow crack we'd managed to open, but he couldn't fit Nebbezim's birdcage through the opening. It dangled from his fingers and banged against the wall as he struggled.

"Help, Connor! I can't fit Lord Nebbezim through the doorway," Simon pleaded.

If not for the danger all around, I might have laughed. Simon mistakenly believed that I was still under Nebbezim's hypnosis.

The birdcage was mine to take.

"The door!" Nebbezim shrieked. The whispering sound was gone from his voice. "Open the door!"

Feeling triumphant, I snatched the cage and easily pried it from Simon's grasp. He howled in dismay from the other side of the door.

"Traitor!" he screamed.

But I wasn't listening. In one motion, I grabbed the cage and swung it around like a weapon.

As I whirled, it *thronked* into the side of a skeleton's greyish skull. Like a ball on a post, the skeleton's head came free and spun through the air. Its body collapsed instantly in a clattering heap.

Halfway through the swing, I let go of the birdcage and scrambled toward the door.

For one brief second I saw Nebbezim staring at me in rage as he and the cage flew into the ranks of the skeletons. His yellow eyes blazed and his hourglass tattoo seemed to pulse like a vein.

One word echoed in my mind.

Death...eath.

Then I slipped past the door and slammed it shut.

Trapped!

21

Simon was on top of me almost immediately. "What have you done?" he roared accusingly.

I grabbed him by the shoulders and shook him roughly. "Simon, relax! Think about Nebbezim. Think about what he *is*."

I hoped Simon would listen. Earlier when I'd rested on the stairs away from the birdcage, I'd come to my senses. Maybe Simon could, too, now that Nebbezim was trapped on the other side of the door.

"But…" he protested, struggling weakly. "Lord Nebbezim…."

Suddenly he sagged to the floor with his face buried in his hands. When he looked at me again, tears streaked his cheeks.

"Connor, what have we done?" he breathed quietly. His red hair was more of a mess than usual.

I sighed in relief. Simon was himself again.

"Nothing," I smiled at him. "We *almost* helped a dead necromancer come back to life, but we didn't."

Simon shook his head vigorously. "No, no. I should never have let myself be fooled like that. What kind of wizard am I?"

"The peasant kind," I teased, but Simon didn't laugh.

He climbed back to his feet. "You're missing the point," he said. "Didn't you recognize the tattoo on Nebbezim's head?"

The red tattoo had seemed familiar, but I couldn't place it. It was shaped like an hourglass....

I shrugged lamely and Simon rolled his eyes. "Sir Filabard's ring. The tattoo looks exactly like the jewel on the ring."

My mouth fell open. Simon was right! The shape and color of the tattoo matched Sir Filabard's ring exactly. That meant—

"Sir Filabard is trying to free Nebbezim," I blurted in understanding. "That's why he brought us all here. Not for treasure. For Nebbezim."

Simon nodded his head and snickered. "I guess you can think with something other than muscle after all."

I poked him in the ribs and we laughed until a scrape and thump came from the door. The skeletons were trying to break through.

Without a word, we threw down the thick wooden bar used to lock the door then started walking along the passageway.

Unlike the door below, this one hadn't led to a room. We were in an empty hall lit dimly by a pale glow in the distance.

Tiptoeing quietly, we crept down the hall. There was something in the tower that could bring a dead wizard back to life. We didn't want it to find us before we found it.

The hall ended with doors to our right and left. A short window opened in the wall straight ahead. The faint glow came from beyond it.

I glanced curiously at the window then shrugged. I guess it wasn't all that surprising to find a window in a tower. If the castle was above ground, it would be normal to see windows in all of its towers.

Then I had another thought. *Maybe the castle had been above ground long ago. Why else would it have even one window?*

Simon grabbed my arm before I gripped the handle to the door on the left. "Wait," he urged. "What are we doing?"

I squinted at him with a puzzled look on my face. "What do you mean? We're escaping from Nebbezim."

"No, I meant, what's our plan?" he explained. "Act Ninety-Seven. *Action Without Thought Tempts Peril.*"

When I kept squinting, he continued. "Think about where we are, Connor. A tower. How do we get out?"

Stairs, I answered silently and my eyes widened in understanding. Nebbezim and the skeletons had us trapped in the tower. We couldn't get past them to the stairs.

We had to find another way out.

"How are we going to get away from here?" I asked.

Simon's eyes glanced from me to the window and I knew exactly what he was thinking.

The only escape was to climb out the window.

Have a Good Flight

22

To my astonishment, Simon leaned so dangerously far out the window that I feared he was going to jump or fall. I grabbed the hood of his robe and hauled him back inside.

"Are you insane?" I hadn't really expected an answer but couldn't resist asking either.

"I just wanted a look at the bottom," he shrugged then started to rummage for something in his pockets.

I waited for him to say more, but he didn't. "And what did you see, peasant?" I asked, a little annoyed.

"Hmm? Oh, nothing," he muttered. "Not the bottom anyway. It's too far down."

I grunted. Simon's words didn't make me feel any better. We had an undead wizard behind us and a bottomless pit in front.

"Aha!" Simon cheered and pulled two oily black feathers from a pocket on his sleeve. "Here, take one," he said.

I took the feather and stared at it doubtfully. It reminded

me of Nebbezim's ravens and I decided that it was probably best if I didn't ask where Simon had gotten it.

"Now, whatever you do, don't let go," he told me seriously. "Hang on to it for as long as it takes."

My stomach tightened and I suddenly couldn't swallow because my throat was so dry. I had a bad feeling about what Simon expected us to do. "We're going to jump out of the window, aren't we?"

In response, Simon grabbed my arm and tugged me toward the window. "Sit on the edge, please, but don't move. I'll let you know when it's time to jump."

I blinked. Simon really did plan on jumping!

But I went to the window without another question or complaint. If Simon wasn't afraid, I couldn't let him think I was. I climbed onto the ledge then carefully sat with my legs dangling over the edge.

A huge, dark cavern opened below and above me. I couldn't see any walls, ceiling, or floor. There was only the soft white glow far below.

"Hurry, please," I whispered, but doubted that Simon heard. He was behind me softly chanting a simple rhyme.

Float, feather, float,
Gentle and light.
Fall, Connor, fall,
Have a good flight.

Simon finished the verse then cleared his throat. I expected him to chant again but more words never came.

He tickled my ear with his feather, then shoved me hard in the back.

"Simon!" I screamed in panic and disbelief. Was he trying to kill me?

I flailed my arms and legs wildly but it was too late. I'd already lost my balance. My backside slipped from the ledge and I fell.

Wind howled in my ears and the outer wall of the tower sped by. My stomach flew up into my throat.

Simon had betrayed me and I was going to die. Why would he do that? Was he still under Nebbezim's spell?

Spinning helplessly, I spotted Simon peering out from the window above. His face grew smaller and smaller as I raced toward my death.

"Hold your breath!" he cried. "To slow down, hold your breath!"

I realized then that I was screaming and snapped my mouth shut. I squeezed the feather as tightly as I could in both hands.

And a wondrous thing happened.

I slowed down.

The wind rushing by me died and I felt like I was drifting on a raft over a calm lagoon.

I wasn't going to die and Simon hadn't tricked me. His magic had saved me. I was floating just like the feather in my hands would float.

Wizards are amazing, I realized. Not as amazing as knights, but still pretty good to have around. I was glad that Simon was my friend even if he was a peasant.

For the next several minutes, I floated silently down. It would have been lonely if I hadn't known Simon was floating above. In the silence, I lost track of time and felt like I was the only living thing in the world.

Eventually the pale light brightened as I neared the bottom. When my feet gently touched the ground, I exhaled and dropped my feather.

From above, I heard a long, joyful squeal. It sounded like a young kid playing with a new puppy.

I squinted up to see Simon spinning his arms and kicking his legs crazily. His robe flapped about him like a flag in the wind.

He was falling too fast!

"Huzzaaaahhhhh!" he cried, and I realized he was falling fast on purpose. Now that was brave. And a little bit nuts.

At the last possible moment, Simon stopped shouting and floated lazily down from about ten feet above me. He landed with a soft thump.

"Wasn't that fun?" he beamed. His face was flushed with excitement.

But I didn't have time to answer.

The ground rumbled violently and we tumbled over.

From a passage across the cavern slithered the biggest creature I'd ever seen. It was shaped like a worm but had two long, pinkish antennae sticking up from its head. It was white and glowed like the walls of the cavern.

"Run!" I shouted, scrambling to my feet, but Simon didn't need to be told. He was already sprinting ahead.

If we didn't hurry, the worm would crush us.

SCRENCH

23

S-C-R-E-N-C-H!

Guh-gung, guh-gung, guh-gung.

The worm stretched its massive bulk forward then its midsection and tail slithered heavily to catch up.

S-C-R-E-N-C-H, it stretched again.

It wasn't going to stop for us. I wasn't even sure if it could see us. It didn't have eyes that I could tell.

Simon stumbled ahead of me, tripping over loose rocks and small boulders. He was trying to hurry but just wasn't coordinated enough. I caught him by the sleeve and dragged him along with me.

Guh-gung, guh-gung, guh-gung.

The worm rumbled ponderously on. It wasn't having any trouble crossing the uneven cavern floor. It glided through the rocks like a rowboat through a patch of lily pads.

A wide tunnel opened in the wall ahead of us. Briefly I thought about circling back around the worm in the hopes that it would pass us on its way to the tunnel, but that was too risky.

We had to keep going. If the worm didn't enter the tunnel, it could easily corner us against a wall.

S-C-R-E-N-C-H!

We staggered side-by-side through the mouth of the tunnel like teammates in a three-legged race. I had my hand on Simon's arm and he clutched desperately to the back of my doublet.

Darkness filled the tunnel and forced us to slow down. When Simon tripped and fell, we stopped to catch our breath.

Behind us the glow of the cavern dimmed as the worm slithered into the tunnel. We didn't have long to rest.

"What about magic?" I asked, panting hard. "Can you use it to scare the worm or make us invisible—anything?"

Guh-gung, guh-gung, guh-gung.

Simon shook his head weakly. "I'm sorry, Connor," he apologized. "I'm too tired. I wasn't even sure my feather spell would work twice."

I gulped at that. Simon had sent me out the window first. That meant he'd risked himself to save me. If his magic had failed, he would have been trapped in Nebbezim's tower alone.

And he hadn't said a word of it to me, just like Act Ten taught knights to do:

Act Out of Charity and Compassion, Not in the Pursuit of Reward or Praise.

Simon really was a knight even if he didn't think so.

S-C-R-E-N-C-H!

Simon deserved my thanks, but we didn't have time to waste. The worm was getting close.

I grabbed his sleeve again and turned to hurry down the tunnel.

Guh-gung, guh-gung, guh-gung.

The worm was only about twenty feet away. Its antennae pulsed threateningly with a deep red light.

"Wait!" Simon hissed, planting his feet. "We'll never outrun it."

"Do you have a better idea?" I shot back quickly, still trying to pull him ahead. The worm was so close now that the red glow of its antennae reflected eerily like blood on Simon's face.

"Yes," he said, pointing at the wall.

I should have known better than to ask. Simon always seemed to have good ideas.

He pointed at a small niche in the tunnel's wall. It was shallow and narrow but probably big enough for both of us.

We backed in awkwardly and stood panting and sweating with rocks poking into our backs. Simon's elbow jabbed into my side, but all I could do was try to ignore it.

And wait for the worm.

As it slithered nearer, I realized it was even bigger than I'd thought. It rose over ten feet and measured at least three times as long.

S-C-R-E-N-C-H, it passed so close that we could reach out to touch its spongy skin.

We didn't do that, of course.

Hardly breathing, I counted silently to fifty before the worm's tail snaked into view. That's when I noticed something slung over its back like a saddle on a horse.

It was a large basket made of woven vines. It hung down over the worm's sides.

Now how did that get there, I wondered.

"That's our way out," Simon said confidently.

I tried to face him but couldn't in the cramped space of the niche. "What do you mean?"

"The basket," he said. "Whoever put it there can probably help us get back to the surface."

Before I could respond, he squirmed out of the niche and started chasing after the worm.

I sighed but quickly followed. Chasing the worm probably wasn't one of Simon's good ideas, but it was too late to stop him.

We caught the worm as it slowed to turn down a branching tunnel. Running beside it, I gritted my teeth, leaped, and grabbed the basket on my first try. Compared to catching Simon's throne in mid-air, this was easy.

But Simon wasn't having the same luck.

Being shorter than me and less coordinated, his jumps weren't very accurate. He'd leap, flail his arms, and then tumble to the ground with a grunt.

It looked like he was trying to fly and I had to bite my tongue to keep from laughing and losing my grip.

On his fifth jump, I yelped in pain when his fingernails dug into my leg.

"Sorry!" he gasped without letting go.

"Just hurry," I grimaced. I didn't want to say it, but if he hung onto my leg too long, he would pull my hose right off.

Now how would that look? Me dangling from the side of a worm while wearing no pants. I'd never heard of an Act in the *Noble Deeds and Duties* to cover that.

Using me as a ladder, Simon struggled onto my shoulders then toppled into the basket. He managed to kick me in the head only once.

"Oof," he grunted as he landed. The impact almost knocked me loose, but Simon leaned over the edge to offer me his hand. As the worm built up speed, I hoisted myself up and dropped down next to him.

We were both exhausted. Even miles underground in a basket on the back of a giant worm, it was nice to finally sit. So much had happened and there was no telling how long we'd been awake.

In minutes, the deep, rumbling and rocking motion of the worm lulled us to sleep.

Bright Eyes and Apples

24

I dreamed of floating through darkness filled with music. Clear, high voices sang happily as I drifted along. When their song ended, I opened my eyes.

I was still in the basket, but the worm had stopped moving. Simon snored softly across from me and I nudged him awake with my toe.

"We stopped," I whispered. "It's time to see if you were right." I meant about his idea for finding help.

He nodded sleepily, stretched, then cupped an ear with one hand like he was listening for something.

I held my breath and listened, too. A rhythmic metallic sound chimed nearby. It sounded like Mr. Sootbeard pounding on his forge.

Ding-ting-ting, the sound echoed like the ringing of a tiny bell.

Motioning for Simon to stay quiet, I slowly raised my head and peered out of the basket.

We were in a glowing cavern with walls as smooth as glass. The glow came from inside the walls like it was trapped there.

Ding-ting-ting.

A group of strange little people clustered along the far wall with their backs to us. They swung tiny mining tools against the wall and sang to the rhythm of their blows. It was the same song I'd heard in my dream.

The people's tiny voices matched their tiny bodies. They were barely as tall as Simon and had long, colorful hair of crystal blue, silver, and emerald.

I couldn't remember ever seeing anyone like them, but they seemed familiar somehow. Their cheerful song convinced me that they were friendly, so I decided to have a closer look.

Before Simon could stop me, I climbed from the basket and dropped to the ground with a thud. The noise echoed loudly throughout the cavern.

The tiny people instantly stopped singing and swinging their tools. As quick as cats, they spun around.

I gasped. Their big, round eyes sparkled like gems the same color as their hair. Looking at them was like looking at a sky of colorful stars.

When the people saw me, their bright eyes widened and they started blabbering questions at me so quickly that I could barely understand them.

"Which-season-is-it?" the first one squeaked rapidly.

"Is-snow-still-cold-and-white?" piped another.

"How-many-times-have-you-tasted-rain?" asked a third.

"Do-leaves-still-fall-in-fall?" the fourth chimed.

Their odd questions kept coming so I held up my hands and smiled. I wanted them to know I was friendly but that I couldn't possibly keep up.

"Please slow down," I begged. I'd never heard people talk so fast. Their words all ran together and their questions didn't make much sense. How could I remember how many times I'd tasted rain?

Thump. Simon dropped down next to me and the little people gasped.

"Apples!" they chirped in astonishment.

Simon was juggling again. First three apples, then four, then five. One for each of the little people. His hands were a blur as he tossed and caught the fruit and pulled more from his robes.

Just how big are his pockets? I asked myself.

"Apples! Apples!" the tiny people exclaimed repeatedly. They crowded around Simon like he was passing out presents.

With quick flicks of his wrist, he nimbly tossed an apple to each person in his audience. They caught them and squealed with joy.

"Thank-you, thank-you!" they beamed.

After Simon delivered the last of his apples, he smiled and gave a low bow. The audience applauded and cheered.

"You-must-come-with-us," one of the people said. He had a pointy blue beard trimmed in a perfect triangle decorated with gleaming crystals.

"Yes-yes, come-with-us," another added. "Bring-your-apples-to-the-king."

Apples to the king? I wondered silently. Only important people met kings, not kids like us. Why were these people so excited about apples?

25

Swallowing hard, I met the sparkling eyes of the tiny people. "Are we your prisoners?" I tried to smile and sound friendly, but I'm not sure I pulled it off.

All at once the people stopped what they were doing and blinked their large eyes. Then they tugged their beards and giggled. The sound reminded me of tinkling wind chimes.

"Glimmers!" squeaked the man with the pointy blue beard. "Forgive-our-manners. What-you-must-think-of-us. What-you-must-think!"

The others shuffled their feet and stared at the floor.

"I-am-Enunarumu, Foregnome-of-the-Crystal-Corps-Miners," the man went on. "Please-call-me-Enu. My-men-and-I-are-gnomes-and-we-are-very-pleased-to-meet-such-extraordinary-guests."

I exhaled loudly and heard Simon do the same. *Guests* sounded a whole lot better than *prisoners*.

It was also nice to know the names of our new friends.

They were gnomes and Enu was their leader. *Gnomes* rhymes with *homes* and has a silent *g*.

Simon stepped forward and offered his hand to Enu. "I am Simon and this is Connor. We're from Tiller's Field." He pointed up. "That's....umm...up there somewhere."

All of the gnomes gawked at Simon's raised finger.

"Opensky," Enu smiled. "We-know."

Simon raised an eyebrow at me. "*Opensky*?" he mouthed. But I just shrugged. I didn't know what the gnomes were talking about either.

None of the gnomes explained what they meant. Instead they packed their equipment into the basket on the worm's back and then climbed aboard themselves.

They called the worm a *slithersaur*, and it wore special saddles across its back. There was room for each of the gnomes and for me and Simon, too.

In almost no time, we were strapped in and slithering toward our meeting with the gnome king.

If I'd thought the passages and stairs of Castle Burrowfar were confusing, the tunnels were worse. We slithered through tunnel after twisting tunnel and cavern after sprawling cavern.

One cavern was so large that we couldn't see the other side. Pointy stalactites hung from the ceiling like icicles. A *stalactite* is a cone-shaped rock that forms where water and minerals trickle down from above.

In the middle of the cavern was a dark lake. Its waters

didn't stir but I got a creepy feeling that something was watching us. Something unfriendly.

I think the gnomes did, too. They got very quiet and their big eyes darted back and forth as we slithered through the cavern.

When we finally entered a new tunnel, they exhaled softly and started to talk again. Simon leaned close to me and whispered, "They don't like that lake."

I nodded to him, then curiosity got the best of me. "Is there something wrong with the lake?" I asked Enu.

The chatting gnomes snapped their mouths shut and looked apprehensively at their leader.

"Fleshfeast Flood," Enu said while tugging at his pointy beard.

"What does that mean?" I questioned. "Is Fleshfeast Flood the name of the lake?"

Enu nodded slowly. His bright, sapphire-like eyes seemed to dim. "The-lake-is-place-of-great-danger. One-drop-of-its-waters-can-melt-the-skin-from-your-bones."

"What—?" I started to ask but a sharp jab in my ribs cut me short. It was Simon. The look he gave me told me to be quiet.

A huge door appeared from the darkness in front of us. It was solid crystal and stood at least fifty feet tall.

As we approached, Enu drew a tiny whistle on a thin chain from around his neck and gave it a soft blow. The whistle was crystal, too, and pulsed with energy.

The door flashed brightly and started to hum. Then it opened.

I gazed at the door in amazement. Like the crystals in the caverns, it seemed alive. Light swirled beneath its bright surface.

As we passed through, Enu stood in his saddle and spread his arms wide. He smiled at me and Simon, his eyes sparkling again.

"Welcome-to-Deephome-Glimmering, our-home-away-from-home" the gnome announced. "Behold-wonders-wrought-in-exile. Behold-the-marvel-of-our-crystals."

I tried to speak but the words got stuck in my throat.

A huge cavern opened below us like a valley. It glowed so brightly with crystals that I almost forgot we were underground.

Crystal buildings and paved crystal streets covered the floor of the valley like a city ten times the size of Tiller's Field.

People filled the streets. Slithersaurs wiggled here and there. Houses and shops stood in orderly rows.

But what caught my eye was an enormous castle in the center of the city. It was several stories tall and had at least a dozen shining crystal towers that soared into the air.

"What's that place?" I asked, pointing at the wondrous building.

Enu smiled again. "The-jewel-among-jewels," he said proudly. "It-is-New-Burrowfar. Palace-of-King-

Ogogiyargo-and-his-lovely-daughter-Princess-Otoonuoti."

I blinked in surprise. Why would the palace be called New Burrowfar? Burrowfar was the name of Nebbezim's haunted castle. Simon had read the name on the entry tower's door.

New concerns crept into my mind. Could the two castles be connected? Were the gnomes friends with Nebbezim?

"Enjoy-the-view," Enu added after a moment of silence. "We-arrive-there-soon."

Gnomefriend

26

Everything for the next few minutes was a blur. The brilliant sights of the city whisked by as we slithered toward the palace of New Burrowfar.

Gnomes stared at me and Simon from everywhere. From street corners, from windows, and from the backs of slithersaurs. The attention made me a little nervous, but not one of the gnomes gave us a dirty look.

They actually seemed glad to see us. Maybe even relieved. Like they'd been waiting for us.

Enu guided our slithersaur through a wide, arched opening in the palace's outer wall and into a slithersaur stable.

The stable was a long cave lit by glowing crystals that hung from the ceiling. Short fences formed slithersaur corrals and in the middle of each corral was a tunnel.

Enu gave his mining crew some instructions then led Simon and me into a narrow shaft in one wall. A large wheel with a glittering handle stuck up from the center of the floor.

"Stand-back-and-hold-in-your-toes," Enu grinned, pointing at the wheel. "Just-a-few-quick-turns-and-we-will-be-in-the-palace."

Simon and I glanced at the wheel then at each other. What did the gnome mean?

Enu chuckled at us as he grabbed the wheel's handle and spun it round and round.

Suddenly the floor trembled, sending me and Simon sprawling. In front of us, the exit dropped away as the whole shaft lurched upward.

My stomach rolled and I threw my arms out against the walls. "What's happening?" I cried.

The gnome giggled. "First-time-in-an-up-down, eh? Guess-you-do-not-use-them-so-much-in-Opensky."

Simon and I both shook our heads frantically. "What does it do—an updown?" Simon asked between clenched teeth.

"Why, it-takes-you-up-or-down, of-course!" Enu laughed merrily. "Wheeeee!"

There was a loud *clunk* from above followed by a soft *snick* and we stopped moving. Enu waved us toward a new opening that had appeared in the wall.

A passage of polished marble stretched ahead. Enu started down it, and we followed quickly, our boots clicking on the smooth floor.

We stopped before a set of crystal double doors like we'd

seen in Nebbezim's castle.

"Please-wait-here," Enu requested, "until-I-introduce-you. All-the-gnomes-have-been-waiting-a-very-long-time-to-meet-you. A-very-long-time. There-is-no-need-to-rush-now-that-you-are-here."

"Waiting…?" I started to ask, but Enu swung the doors open and stepped through before I could finish.

In a loud voice, he announced our arrival. "Pardon-the-rude-intrusion, my-king, but-I-am-delighted-to-introduce-wondrous-guests-from-Opensky."

We heard a gasp of many voices and one or two exclamations of "Glimmers!" before Enu spoke again.

"I-present-Sir-Connor-Gnomefriend-the-Curious," he called and my heart froze.

Did he mean me? I wasn't ready! What should I do? I'd never met a king before.

Simon shoved me in the back. "Get going, *Gnomefriend*," he snickered.

I socked him lightly on the shoulder then shuffled woodenly through the doors before I thought anymore about what I was doing.

A short flight of stairs led to a large, familiar room. It took me a second to place it, but I recognized the stone columns and raised platform on the far side.

The room looked exactly like the throne room in Castle Burrowfar where we'd found the flying thrones.

A crowd of gnomes cheered and applauded as I entered.

Some sat on small thrones. Others leaned on crystal staffs. All of them looked excited and beamed at me.

I started to fidget and sweat.

"Now-I-present," Enu chirped, "Sir-Simon-Fruitgiver-of-Red-Orchard."

A strange thing happened next. The crowd went impossibly still. In the silence, I imagined I could hear beads of sweat trickling down my forehead.

Simon stumbled down the steps to stand next to me, and the long, uncomfortable silence continued. It felt like when an adult sits you down for a lecture and you're waiting for it to begin.

Eh-eh-kerchoooo!

A gnome sneezed wetly and loudly.

High-pitched laughter broke out all over the room. Gnomes held their bellies, tugged their beards, and bent over in fits of giggles.

Confused but relieved, Simon and I joined in. We weren't sure why a sneeze was so funny, but laughing seemed like the thing to do. We didn't want to insult our new friends.

A chubby gnome dressed in a silvery robe and crown stood and held up his pudgy hands. He had a ruby red beard and hair.

The laughter slowly quieted and the round man smiled.

"Delighted-greetings-and-heartfelt-welcomes-to-New-Burrowfar," he said to us in squeaky gnome fashion. "I-am-Ogo, king-of-the-gnome-exiles-and-Deephome-

Glimmering."

Simon and I stood up a little straighter. A king was talking to us. We were supposed to show respect.

"Now," King Ogo continued with a serious look on his face. "Which-of-you-is-here-to-marry-my-daughter?"

Princess Oti

27

"*DADDY!*"

A girl's blood-curdling shriek made the hairs on the back of my neck stand up straight.

All eyes in the room turned as a tiny gnome pushed her way through the crowd to stand before the king.

The girl had short purple hair and wide purple eyes. She wore a long pale green tunic belted at the waist like a dress and had her hands balled into fists at her sides.

She was beyond furious.

"Daddy, how-could-you?" she demanded with a stomp of her foot.

Simon and I took a step back. Somehow the room seemed to have shrunk. We couldn't get far enough away from King Ogo and his enraged daughter.

Surprisingly Enu nudged me with his elbow and winked. "Princess-Otoonuoti," he whispered from one corner of his mouth. "She-is-very-excitable-and-the-king-enjoys-this-game."

Game? I wondered doubtfully. The princess didn't look like she was enjoying herself.

But then a silly grin tickled the king's chubby cheeks and he let out a barking sort of laugh. He shrugged innocently.

The princess scowled back at him playfully and poked his round belly with a finger. The anger had vanished from her face.

"You-are-a-bad-man, daddy," she teased. "May-slithersaurs-infest-your-bath-water!" Then she stood on her tiptoes and kissed him on the cheek.

The other gnomes in the room exhaled and then smiled or laughed. They must not have been sure the princess was playing a game.

I wondered what that said about her.

With a flourish, she spun around to face me and Simon. "Greetings, brave-heroes-from-Opensky," she squeaked, curtsying low. "I-am-Princess-Otoonuoti. On-behalf-of-all-gnomes, I-welcome-you-to-New-Burrowfar."

There was that name again. *Burrowfar*. Why would the gnomes pick the same name as Nebbezim's castle?

"Come-with-me, please," the princess continued, "to-enjoy-the-hospitality-of-humble-gnomes. You-must-be-famished-from-your-travels."

Although it was hard for me to hear all of her quick words, I understood enough of them. She was talking about feeding us.

It was the best idea I'd heard in a long time.

Almost too fast to follow, the princess skipped down from the throne platform and across the room. With a mischievous wink, she caught Simon and me by the elbow and tugged us toward the exit.

As we turned to leave, King Ogo spoke. "Be-sure-not-to-eat-all-of-their-apples, daughter," he cautioned.

For some reason, the comment made the crowd giggle nervously. The gnomes were sure interested in apples.

Through the door and back in the hall, the princess pulled us around to face her. Her big purple eyes sparkled with excitement.

"We-must-hurry," she whispered, "before-anyone-suspects-our-plan."

I blinked. Was eating some kind of secret?

"What plan?" I asked, and Simon nodded. He didn't understand what she was talking about either.

The princess cocked her head at me. "The-plan-to-return-to-Opensky," she said as if she was explaining swimming to a fish.

We squinted at her. "Opensky?" Simon asked.

She rolled her eyes. "Opensky," she chirped, pointing straight up. "The-surface. Up-there. You-do-plan-on-returning-to-your-home? Glimmers!"

Simon and I nodded. The only reason we were in the gnome city was to find a guide to the surface. We had to stop Sir Filabard from bringing Nebbezim back to life.

"Well-so-do-I," the princess vowed. "We-gnomes-have-been-trapped-down-here-for-centuries. We-miss-the-sun, the-stars, the-seasons...."

She trailed off as a faraway look crept into her eyes, and the pause allowed me to figure something out.

The gnomes didn't live down here by choice. They used to live on the surface just like me and Simon.

I'm not sure why I hadn't realized it before. The signs were obvious. The gnomes had named their castle *New* Burrowfar after their old home.

It made such simple sense.

And horrifying, too.

"Nebbezim turned your people to stone," I said quietly. It wasn't a question. I knew I was right. The child-sized statues we'd seen in Nebbezim's castle looked too much like gnomes.

"Shhh!" the princess hissed. "Never-say-that-terrible-name-here."

She grabbed our elbows again and dragged us down the hall. "We-will-talk-more-outside, but-we-must-be-quick-now. We-cannot-allow-anyone-to-know-where-we-are-going."

I didn't want to ask, but at the same time I had to. "Where *are* we going?"

The princess cleared her throat. "Fleshfeast-Flood, of-course. It-is-the-only-way-to-the-surface."

My knees felt suddenly weak. Enu had told us that

Fleshfeast Flood was a lake of acid. One touch of its magical waters could kill us.

Slithersaur Challenge

28

"Now-get-one-thing-straight," the princess told us with her hands on her hips. "My-name-is-Otoonuoti."

She said it really slowly.

O-too-nu-o-ti.

"Got-it?" she asked, eyeing us carefully.

"Um, sure, Princess O-tuna," I replied smartly with a straight face.

Simon snickered. "No, no," he said, "it's Princess O-tuba-tune." He snickered again.

The princess didn't look amused. "Fine-then, call-me-Oti. *Princess*-Oti." The way she emphasized *princess* made it sound all business. Like we'd better remember to use it or else.

I bowed low. "As you wish, princess."

Oti flicked me on the ear while my head was down. Then she muttered something under her breath that I couldn't quite catch, but it sounded a lot like "peasants."

I decided to keep my eyes on Princess Oti. She was going to be trouble, I just knew it.

From there we hurried down the long hall and into the up-down. Oti didn't say anything but gave the wheel a hard spin that sent us racing downward. Harder than necessary, I think.

When Simon and I lost our balance and stumbled, Oti smiled and rocked back on her heels. She looked as smug as a cat with two mice trapped in a corner.

Back in the slithersaur stable, Oti led us to a large but empty corral. We climbed the short fence and went inside.

As I could have guessed, Simon got his robes caught on a fence post and tripped. Luckily Oti didn't seem to notice. She was concentrating on the tunnel opening in the center of the corral.

"Be careful," I grumbled quietly at Simon. "We can't give her any excuses."

"Excuses for what?" Simon blinked at me.

"You know, to act like...." I flailed my arms while trying to think of the right words. "To act like a spoiled princess."

Simon's hair flopped as he shook his head. "I don't know what you're talking about." Then he scampered ahead to join Oti.

I couldn't keep from rolling my eyes. Simon had a crush on the princess! Now they'd both be trouble.

One word summed it up.

Peasants.

Oti had her eyes closed and was whistling softly. The sound fluttered up and down from high to low. It made my ears tingle.

"Be-still-now," Oti said. "Opal-is-shy. Your-big-human-stomping-and-huffing-and-puffing-might-frighten-her."

Big human stomping? I wondered irritably. *Just what did that mean?*

I was about to snap at her when two red antennae peeked from the tunnel. They wobbled back and forth, darting this way and that the way a dog investigates different smells. Then slowly a slithersaur wiggled into view.

It was the smallest I'd seen, about half the size of Enu's and only as tall as me. It wore a polished red saddle decorated by a fancy red ribbon.

"It's kind of puny," I teased Oti. "Are you sure it can carry all three of us?"

"Hush," Oti squeaked. "*She*-is-not-an-it. Her-name-is-Opal, and-she-can-carry-plenty. Even-human-lugs-like-you."

Oti gently patted the slithersaur's side and whispered something I couldn't hear. The soothing sound made my ears tingle again.

There was something odd about Oti's voice. About all gnome voices.

As if to prove my suspicions, Oti let out a short shout and vaulted suddenly into Opal's saddle in one great leap.

It was an amazing jump with no running start or boost up.

One second she was standing next to the slithersaur, the next she was whizzing up in the air and right onto Opal's back. Not once did her flailing arms touch anything but air until she landed.

I just knew her shout had something to do with the jump. It had to be magic. No one could leap straight into the air like that without help.

In the saddle, Oti fussed with her purple hair, then smiled down at me and Simon.

"Coming?" she asked with a bored look on her face.

It was a challenge if I'd ever heard one.

Slowly I took a few steps back to measure up the slithersaur. It wasn't big as slithersaurs go, but it was still a long way up.

I sucked in a deep breath and ran. Just before I crashed into the slithersaur's side, I jumped and stretched for its saddle. My hand brushed it, grasping, and I twisted in mid-leap.

Ungh! I grunted as my stomach collided with the slithersaur.

But I'd made it. With a big gesture, I swung my legs over the sides and righted myself in the saddle as far behind Oti as possible.

I'd faced her challenge and won.

"How's that?" I panted.

Oti shrugged and turned to Simon. "Need-a-hand, Simon-of-Red-Orchard?" she chirped sweetly.

I could have spat! Princess Oti wasn't playing by the rules. When one knight bested another, both were supposed to acknowledge the skills of the other.

Act Twenty-seven of the *Noble Deeds and Duties* said:

Be Humble in Victory and Gracious in Defeat.

Shouldn't the Acts teach knights *and* princesses how to behave?

No one said another word as Oti coaxed the slithersaur into the tunnel in the middle of its corral. In no time we left the stable behind and slithered through heavy darkness.

Fleshfeast Flood waited for us, but I couldn't help wondering if Princess Oti would be more trouble than a whole ocean of acid.

Shard Spider Surprise

29

The ride through the tunnel got a little spooky. It was dark. It was long. It was with sassy Princess Oti in the lead.

The only sounds were our anxious breathing and the *scrench, guh-gung, guh-gung* of the slithersaur.

Finally, I couldn't take anymore. "How long is this tunnel?" I blurted and immediately wished I hadn't.

Ahead of me, Oti giggled musically.

I could have bit my tongue in frustration. Oti would pounce all over my concern.

Two large purple eyes focused on me from the dark. "You-are-not-afraid-of-the-dark, are you?" Oti asked, sounding like a mother talking to a two-year old. "Or-of-being-trapped-in-small-spaces?"

Not normally, no, I thought. But just then the dark looked a little darker and the tunnel a little smaller. It felt like everything around us was shrinking.

"No—" I started defensively, but Simon interrupted.

"I'm eager to get out," he admitted.

Good old Simon. He'd come to my rescue. Maybe he'd finally realized that Princess Oti needed a lesson or two in manners.

Long lessons.

"It-will-not-be-too-much-longer," Oti promised, "but-perhaps-I-can-make-you-more-comfortable."

There was a short pause followed by the snap of fingers. "I know!" Oti squeaked excitedly, then she recited a ridiculous poem.

Connor-Connor, do-not-cry.
Wipe-those-tears
From-your-eyes.
Princess-power, princess-might,
Makes-you-brave.
Have-no-fright.

The poem went on from there, but it didn't get any better. Each verse was about scaredy-cat me and brave Princess Oti. She pumped her arms to the beat like she was marching in a parade.

The poem was actually pretty funny, but I'd never admit that out loud.

The strangest thing about it, I really did feel better while Oti warbled the silly words in a nursery rhyme sort of way. My ears tingled warmly and I forgot about the suffocating closeness of the dark, narrow tunnel.

Almost without realizing it, we passed out of the tunnel and into a round cavern with five other openings in the walls. Each of the openings was blocked by a round crystal door.

With a high-pitched squeak, Oti drew the slithersaur to a halt and hopped from the saddle. Just like she'd leaped in earlier, she jumped out with little effort.

"We-must-walk-from-here," she said. "The-doorway-is-too-narrow-for-Opal."

"Where are we?" Simon asked, gazing about the cavern. "None of this looks familiar."

Oti giggled and skipped about on her toes. "It-should-not," she piped. "These-doors-are-for-official-princess-use-only."

"So where do they go?" I asked quickly. I didn't want to give Oti time to brag about the privileges of being a princess.

The little gnome girl squinted at me and wiggled her fingers like a spell-casting wizard. "To-secret-places," she said mysteriously. "If-I-told-you, you-would-have-to-marry-me."

She and Simon laughed.

I nearly choked. "Forget I asked."

When she and Simon recovered, Oti turned to face the second door on our left. In a voice that reminded me of a flute, she chanted these words:

Door-without-handle,
Lock, hinge, or-knob—
Open, obey-me.
That-is-your-job.

There came a low humming sound that quickly rose to a high whistle. The door shined brightly, flashed once, and disappeared.

An opening where the door had been led to another tunnel. Faint light shined at its end.

"Almost-there-now," Oti breathed quietly. "Be-quiet-and-keep-your-eyes-open. There-might-be-shard-spiders-about."

Shard spiders?

Simon and I glanced at each other. I hoped he'd recovered enough to use his magic again. Without a weapon, I wasn't going to be much help in a fight.

The three of us entered the tunnel. Behind us, white light flashed, and when I looked over my shoulder, the door had reappeared.

There was nowhere to go but forward. Toward the shard spiders and Fleshfeast Flood.

Luckily, the tunnel wasn't very long and Princess Oti didn't have time to make up more rhymes about me.

We came into a familiar cavern. Mushrooms the size of trees and patches of glowing fungus grew all around. Stalactites dangled from the ceiling like fangs.

Across the cavern the waters of Fleshfeast Flood sparkled.

We'd finally made it. We were on our way home.

"Now how do we...?" I began when a dark shadow passed over my head. I felt it like an icy itch inside my skull.

"Look out!" Simon howled at me, his face deathly pale.

Oti squealed. "Shard-spider!"

I looked up in time to see a bloated crystal body drop down on me from the ceiling. Eight spindly legs twitched hungrily.

The spider was as big as a large dog.

As it crashed onto me and knocked me to the ground, I screamed.

Oti's Song

30

Twitching legs as hard as rock pinned me to the cavern floor. Pincers snapped at my face.

Beneath the shard spider, I desperately flailed my arms and legs, beating against its solid body. I didn't have long before its weight crushed me.

Darkness crowded the edges of my vision and my lungs burned with the need for air.

I was going to pass out.

E-E-E-Y-A-A-H!

A fierce cry as sharp as a sword blade echoed throughout the cavern.

On my chest, the spider trembled once before going perfectly still. Its unmoving legs pressed down on me like fallen tree limbs.

Then the spider exploded.

Crackling like ice under a giant's boot, it shattered in a cloud of white. Bits of crystal pelted me like bee stings, and

I screamed again, but more from surprise than pain.

The spider was gone. Broken into a million pieces.

I gulped a huge breath of air and propped myself up. My body stung in a dozen places, but I was alive.

Simon rushed to my side and helped me to sit. "Are you all right?" he asked worriedly. His eyes were as big as the apples he liked to juggle.

I nodded numbly. I'd be fine once I caught my breath.

A tiny cough came from nearby. It was Princess Oti. She was on her knees with her head down, panting heavily.

"Oti…?" I started to ask then realized something important.

My suspicions about her voice were right. She *could* do magic. The cry I'd heard had been Oti using her voice to destroy the shard spider.

I went to her and gently pulled her to her feet. She didn't say anything and leaned heavily on my arm for support. I could tell she was exhausted.

"Thank you," I told her seriously, but words weren't enough. She'd saved my life. After all the teasing, she'd still saved me.

I owed her everything.

Appreciate the Giver More Than the Gift, read Act Fifty-one. Somehow I knew I'd be able to overlook Princess Oti's faults from then on.

Simon stumbled over. "Was anyone hurt? How about a juicy apple to rebuild your strength?"

Oti's head came up sharply. "Glimmers, no!" she gasped. "Keep-that-safe, please. We-need-it-much-and-soon." Her words were even faster than usual.

Her tone frightened Simon and he gripped the apple protectively in both hands.

Oti then looked at me. The purple of her eyes looked dull and weak. "You-are-very-welcome, Connor-Gnomefriend," she said softly.

I was a little embarrassed by the look she gave me so I changed the subject. "What was that thing?" I asked.

"A-shard-spider," she explained. "A-magical-creation-made-by-Nebbezim. The-spiders-are-not-really-alive, but-they-make-good-guardians."

"And what do they guard?" Simon asked curiously.

Oti sighed. "Fleshfeast-Flood-and-the-way-to-the-surface. The-spiders-are-meant-to-keep-gnomes-away."

Without another word, she turned and started walking toward Fleshfeast Flood. Simon and I had to hurry to catch her.

A cloudy mist hung thickly over the surface of the pool, hiding its far side from view.

"Stand-back-now," Oti requested. "I-must-summon-the-helmsman, Charos."

I get it, I realized. *There must be a gnome ship waiting for us in the mist.*

A *helmsman* is a sailor who steers a ship.

Oti cleared her throat and stood up as tall as she was able.

With her eyes fixed on Fleshfeast Flood, she sang.

Listen to me, growing green.
Listen to me, rain.
Hear my wish for bumble's queen.
I miss spring's refrain.

Spring, summer, winter, fall—
Once for each, once for all.
Round around, lost then found,
The seasons never stall.

Listen to me, butterflies.
Listen to me, sun.
Hear my wish for clear blue skies.
I miss summer's fun.

Spring, summer, winter, fall—
Once for each, once for all.
Round around, lost then found,
The seasons never stall.

Listen to me, chilly breeze.
Listen to me, fall.
Hear my wish for colored leaves.
I miss autumn's call.

Spring, summer, winter, fall—
Once for each, once for all.
Round around, lost then found,
The seasons never stall.

Listen to me, mistletoe.
Listen to me, moon.
Hear my wish for knee-deep snow.
I miss winter's boon

Spring, summer, winter, fall—
Once for each, once for all.
Round around, lost then found,
The seasons never stall.

The notes of Oti's song vanished suddenly as if swallowed by the lake. She stepped back to join us, but did not take her eyes from the water.

Acid, I reminded myself. I kept calling Fleshfeast Flood a lake. If I kept that up, I might learn a deadly lesson the hard way.

Still, the pool looked so calm and inviting....

With a yawn, Simon started forward. "I'm going for a little swim," he muttered drowsily.

It sounded like a good idea to me, too, but a scream bellowed in the back of my mind.

"Simon, no!" I shouted and snagged him by the collar just before he stepped into the pool. The liquid hissed where pebbles trickled into it from his weight.

An echoing laugh that sounded like a snake slithering over something very dry drifted in from the mist, and a boat appeared. Or what used to be a boat. It was a skeleton ship made of wooden beams and supports but no walled sides or bottom.

More surprising, it floated several inches above the pool and made no sound as it came toward us.

A man wearing a deep black robe and hood guided the boat with a long silver staff. The staff touched the pool but made no ripples.

The man and his strange ship were like ghosts gliding lightly over the waters.

As they approached, I saw that the man was very tall and thin. His robes were tattered and hung from his body like a hand-me-down from a much bigger sibling.

His head came up when he reached the shore, and I stumbled back in alarm.

His face was a skinless skull, and eyes shaped like hourglasses burned from inside his hood.

31

"Nebbezim!" I roared, reaching for a weapon that wasn't there.

Simon jumped back a step and dropped into a crouch. His hands and fingers were spread like he was going to cast a spell.

"Stop-stop!" Oti cried. She leaped in front of me and Simon, waving her arms.

"Do-not-attack," she pleaded. "The-helmsman-is-Charos, not-the-evil-wizard. He-is-here-to-take-us-across-Fleshfeast-Flood."

Doubtfully I looked from Oti to the skeleton on the skeletal ship. Its hourglass eyes burned the same red as Filabard's ring and Nebbezim's tattoo.

I was tired of red hourglasses.

If the skeleton wasn't Nebbezim, it still had all of his markings. It could be one of his henchmen. A *henchman* is a servant or follower but not usually the nicest kind to have around.

Oti was wrong to protect the skeleton.

"Stand back, princess," I ordered in my best knight's voice. I tried to grab her arm but she wiggled away.

"Charos, we-seek-passage-to-the-island," she chirped at the robed skeleton.

The creature's dark hood turned slowly and its blazing eyes fixed on us. In a voice that sounded like air seeping through a narrow space, it said:

Black is your sun.
Black is your moon.
Black is your hope down in darkest deep tomb.

Deep will you go.
Deep will you stay.
Deep will you rot beyond light of the day.

When can you leave?
When can you run?
When can you give me a gift from the sun?

One of the skeleton's arms moved up and a bony hand appeared from the end of its robes.

"Your gift," it breathed softly.

"Now, Simon," Oti whispered almost too quietly to be heard. Her eyes didn't move from the skeleton.

Simon groaned in confusion. "N-now what?"

"Your apple. Give it to Charos," she told him.

While Simon fumbled in his pockets, I asked "What good is an apple? That thing is one of Nebbezim's henchmen. We need magic and weapons."

Finally Oti turned away from the skeleton and looked at me. "Did-you-not-listen-to-his-words?"

"Sure I did," I said defensively. "Something about a dark tomb. A riddle."

Oti nodded sadly. "A-riddle, yes, and-a-curse. The-curse-of-the-gnome-people."

The light in her eyes glistened as she continued to speak. She was crying.

"Nebbezim-stole-our-home," she explained, "and-put-a-curse-on-my-people. We-are-trapped-here-miles-under-ground-until—"

"Until," Simon interjected excitedly, "you give Charos something grown in the sun. Like this!"

He thrust his apple in front of us and shook it. "That's what the riddle asked," he added. "'When can you give me a gift from the sun?'"

Oti smiled at him through her tears. "Yes, good-Simon-of-Red-Orchard. Exactly-like-that."

She took the apple carefully like it was made of glass. "No-curse-is-permanent, but Nebbezim-made-his-hard-to-break. Here-in-Deephome-Glimmering, the-sun-is-a-dream. A-memory. We-had-nothing-to-give-Charos."

"Until we arrived," Simon finished proudly.

I finally understood why the gnomes had been so excited

to see apples. It wasn't the apples exactly but something grown in the sun. The gnomes would probably have been as excited to see a stalk of asparagus.

Princess Oti crept toward the pool and got as close to it as possible. With her arm shaking, she gently set the apple into Charos' waiting hand.

The bony fingers snapped shut on the apple like the jaws of a trap and the apple was pulverized. Bits of its skin and fruit dripped into the pool where they were burned to nothing in the steaming, hissing waters.

Charos used his staff to bring his skeletal ship to shore in front of us.

"Boarding now," he rasped.

Fleshfeast Flood

32

The three of us huddled together in the prow of the skeletal ship. The *prow* is the front part of a ship or boat where it curves to a point.

We balanced carefully on the few thin planks along the bottom of the vessel. With our feet wide apart and our hands gripping the rails, we watched the deadly waters of Fleshfeast Flood inch past beneath us.

When we floated into the mist, I tightened my grip. The grey vapor prevented us from seeing more than a few feet in any direction.

To my surprise, Charos spoke. He sounded as casual as a man talking to a neighbor about the weather.

"Where are you headed, travelers?" he asked in his breathy voice.

None of us responded right away. Staring into the mist seemed a thousand times more interesting than talking to a skeleton.

It was impossible to forget that the last skeleton I'd spoken to had used magic and almost gotten me killed.

Finally Simon mumbled, "To the surface." He didn't look at Charos when he said it.

"Ahh, an excellent destination," the skeletal helmsman said. "I long to return there, too, but my shift isn't over."

Distracted by his friendly manner, we all blinked at Charos. "Your-shift?" Oti asked for the three of us.

"Aye, I should be relieved of duty soon," Charos explained, "so that I may go home. My feet are killing me."

The three of us shared confused looks. Where did a skeleton consider home?

Then I thought I understood. "Back to Nebbezim, you mean," I sneered. No matter how friendly Charos acted, his hourglass eyes marked him as one of Nebbezim's henchmen.

Amazingly, Charos chuckled. The breathy sound sent goose bumps darting up my neck.

"Dear me, no," he rasped. "I keep work and my personal life separate."

The skeleton stopped rowing and leaned on his staff. "Actually," he said after a moment, "I'm of a mind to quit this job."

His fiery eyes flashed back and forth like he was afraid someone might overhear our conversation. "It's dreadfully boring work and the shifts are much too long."

What did that mean? I wondered. His feet hurt. He was bored. He wanted to quit his job.

He was acting like he thought of himself as human.

The color drained from my face and I shivered. Maybe Charos was human, or at least used to be. He could be under one of Nebbezim's spells.

"Just how long have you been working?" I forced myself to ask. I was afraid to hear the answer, but I was curious, too.

Charos sighed, sounding like a leak in a balloon. "Eight hundred and ninety two years now."

Princess Oti squeaked. "That-is-exactly-how-long-we-gnomes-have-been-exiled-from-our-home."

Poor Charos.

He'd been used by Nebbezim and probably didn't realize that time and magic had turned him into an undead skeleton.

What a horrible way to live.

"Here we are, friends," the skeleton said. "Funnelspun Isle. Good luck on the rest of your journey." With a thrust of his staff, he guided the boat up to a rocky shoreline.

"Beware the spiders," he added in a hiss.

Funnelspun Isle

33

"I thought we were past the spiders," Simon grumbled as we watched Charos and his ship disappear into the mist from shore.

Oti poked Simon in the ribs and giggled. "You-are-not-afraid-now, too?" She winked at me. "Like-Connor."

I bit my lip but didn't say anything.

Funnelspun Isle was a rocky lump in the middle of Fleshfeast Flood. It rose like a hill up into more thick mist. We couldn't see the top of the hill or the ceiling of the cavern.

"Well, where do we go now?" I asked Oti.

The little princess twirled lightly, her purple eyes darting around the island. "Up, I guess," she finally chirped.

"Up, you *guess*?" I repeated. "You're supposed to be our guide."

She put her hands on her hips and scowled at me. "I-got-us-this-far, did-I-not?" She smirked and pointed high over her head. "The-surface-is-that-way. You-know-as-well-as-I-do."

"But this island," I argued. "You knew it was here. Doesn't that mean you know something about it?"

Oti shook her head rapidly. "Glimmers, no, Sir-Connor-Asks-a-Lot. I-guessed."

"Guessed?" That was the second time she'd used the word.

"About-this-island, silly," she giggled. "A-boat. An-underground-pool. I-guessed-that-we-would-be-taken-to-an-island. Pretty-smart, huh?"

I groaned. We were lost again.

I was about to say something rude, but Simon spoke before I had a chance. "Let's get going. I don't know about you two, but I'm hungry. Charos took my last apple."

We started up the hill and were soon breathing hard. The steep incline and rocks made the going tough. Add that to the fact that my stomach wouldn't stop rumbling, and I was feeling pretty miserable.

Thanks to all the talk about apples.

"What's that?" Simon exclaimed, pointing excitedly up the hill.

Clackity-click-clack.

A dark shape skittered through the mist. Its feet clicked loudly on the stony ground.

It was a shard spider charging from the mist and down the

hill like it was as hungry as me, only it wasn't looking for apples to eat.

The spider was made of the same crystal we'd seen so many times in Deephome-Glimmering. It was whitish and translucent. *Translucent* is a fancy word for mostly see-through.

In the spider's chubby midsection, an eerie red light pulsed rapidly. It was the creature's beating heart.

As brave as any real knight, Simon dashed up the hill toward the spider. He dug furiously in his pockets while he ran.

It was an amazing sight. Sir Simon the Brave rushing forward to protect his friends.

"Aha!" he cheered as he ripped something metal from a pocket. He clutched it in both hands and took a deep breath.

That's when the spider leaped. It bounded above Simon's head and vanished into the mist.

It was gone as silently as a ghost.

"Stay-quiet!" Oti cautioned.

Without a word, we pressed our backs together in a tight circle. The spider would be back but we'd be ready for it.

We waited, panting with nervousness and excitement. Our eyes darted here and there. Into the mist, up the hill, back the way we'd come.

Where had the spider—?

Oti suddenly shrieked and Simon collapsed with a solid

thump. The metal object he'd been holding clattered to the ground.

I spun around in time to see the shard spider bound back into the mist. It had dropped from above to knock Simon over, then fled.

"You all right?" I asked as I helped Simon to stand. He was a little pale but looked unhurt.

"Y-yes," he panted. "Did you see where it went?"

"Up-that-way," Oti said with a nod of her head. Her voice squeaked more than usual and sounded extra fast. "And-I-think-I-know-why."

Simon and I followed her gaze up the hill.

From the mist a dozen shard spiders materialized like phantoms. The red pulsing of their heartbeats reflected against the wall of mist like fire in fog.

Clacking loudly, the arachnid army scuttled downhill.

Ice and Sleet

34

A strange feeling came over me while we waited for the spiders. I felt far away and very calm. The spiders were on their way to kill us, but I wasn't afraid.

I felt like I'd never do anything so important again for the rest of my life.

Sir Filabard and Lord Nebbezim had to be stopped. The two were connected. Sir Filabard's ring and Nebbezim's tattoo told me that much. There was no telling what they were planning.

We had to stop them.

And the spiders were in our way.

"I need a weapon!" I roared more out of frustration than hope.

But as usual, Simon came through.

"I forgot!" he cried. "My hammer." He snatched up the metal object he'd been holding earlier and pushed it into my hands.

It was a small polished hammer about the size of my fist. As I stared at it, cold blue streaks of light flashed across its surface like tiny lightning bolts.

"I need a *real* weapon," I shouted over the noise of the approaching spiders. The hammer was much too small.

But I doubted that Simon heard me. He'd raised his arms and was casting some kind of spell. His voice was loud as he chanted.

Ice and sleet,
Hail and snow.
Winter's magic
Hammer grow!

Howling like a fierce wind, the hammer turned icy cold in my fingers. I gasped and tried to drop the thing, but it was stuck like a person's tongue to a metal post in the winter.

Then the hammer started to swell. It grew and grew.

First it stretched to the length of my arm, then my leg, then my whole body, but I still couldn't let go. It was frozen to my hands.

I gave a cheer and raised the hammer over my head. It felt as light as when Simon had put it in my hands. Only now, it was as long as me and probably twice as wide.

I cheered again. I was invincible!

The spiders were less than ten feet away and I charged.

With a great two-handed swing, I attacked the front line of shard spiders. Snow and stinging bits of ice erupted from the hammer's head with every blow.

Whenever the snow and ice pelted a shard spider, the creature quit moving, frozen solid. A moment later it disintegrated into a harmless mound of snow and slush. All the while, the hammer howled like a storm.

But no matter how many spiders I froze, more appeared. The whole island was alive with them. Their pulsing heartbeats cast eerie red shadows everywhere.

E-E-E-Y-A-A-H! Oti howled next to me and a spider exploded into dust.

"Bug be gone! Say so long!" roared Simon and the spider nearest him rocketed through the air and splashed into Fleshfeast Flood. The hissing waters bubbled and spat as the spider quickly vanished.

Still more spiders came on.

"There's too many!" I shouted after swiping at a shard spider just inches from Oti.

"The ground!" Simon cried. "Strike the hammer on the ground."

I didn't ask why. I just did it. I'd learned to trust Simon and his special talents by then.

From high over my head, I brought the hammer down smack between my feet. The impact knocked all of us to the ground.

There was the blasting boom of a thunderclap and a flash of icy blue light. When I opened my eyes, all of Funnelspun Isle had changed.

A thin sheet of ice covered the island and all of the spiders. Every one of them was frozen stiff.

"Oh-my," Oti squeaked in awe. "How-did-you…?" She didn't finish her question as her eyes took in the amazing sight.

"*Ahem.*" Simon cleared his throat quietly.

We looked at him and he was grinning. His floppy hair was coated with ice and sticking out in every direction.

"And you thought all I could do was juggle," he snickered. Puffs of frost steamed from his mouth.

Then his eyes rolled back into his head and he passed out.

Hammer Hands

35

Oti knelt next to Simon and gently patted his cheek. "Please-wake-up, Simon, wake-up."

"*Ungh*." Simon groaned and fluttered his eyes open. "I put a little too much into that spell," he mumbled.

With Oti's help, he sat up.

"You going to make it?" I asked quickly. Even with the spiders frozen, I didn't want to stick around long.

The magical hammer was starting to melt. Water dripped from its wide head and trickled down my hands and arms. That couldn't be a good sign.

Shaking his head to clear it, Simon said, "We have to hurry. The ice will melt soon."

Drops of water were already appearing on the spiders, and the ground was becoming slushy. I doubted *soon* was the right word.

"Well, what's stopping us?" I asked without expecting an answer.

Oti and Simon got the hint. They climbed to their feet, and we shuffled up the hill.

With the snow and ice melting all around us, the mist became so thick that we could barely see ahead. When the hill leveled off, we figured we'd reached the top.

"Must be as high as it goes," I observed. I peered into the mist but it was like trying to read a book pressed right up against my nose. I just couldn't make anything out.

"Let's keep going but stick close together," Simon suggested. "We don't want to get separated."

"Grab my sleeves and hang on," I added. I still couldn't drop the hammer so holding hands wasn't an option.

We wandered ahead for some time, slipping on the ice and bumping into frozen spiders.

When I ran into the funnel web, we stopped.

A *funnel web* is a special kind of spider's web shaped like a cone. A spider waits inside it, ready to pounce on whatever happens too close.

Seeing it, I realized why the island was named Funnelspun.

In the mist, the web was almost impossible to see. Like the shard spiders, it was made of crystal and was the same translucent white color.

Crisscrossed strands of webbing rose high above us and disappeared overhead. I got the feeling that the funnel went a long way up and was our only way out.

At least it wasn't sticky like a living spider's web.

I pointed up with the shrinking hammer still between my hands. "The surface is that way, right Oti?" I grinned.

She and Simon chuckled but not with much enthusiasm. None of us liked the idea of climbing the funnel.

"Have any feathers left?" I asked Simon. I thought that if his magic could make us float down, it might make us float *up*, too.

He shook his head, spraying drops of water. "We're going to have to climb."

"I-can-help-you-big-footed-lugs," Oti chirped. Her gem-like eyes sparkled playfully.

"Why," I muttered, "do I get the feeling that I won't like your plan?"

"Because-you-do-not-believe-in-princess-power, Connor-the-Grumbler," she giggled. "But-it-will-save-you."

I snorted. "*Sir* Connor the Grumbler," I corrected.

Simon stepped in before our conversation got really out of hand. "Let's just get going. The ice is almost melted."

He was right. My boots were soaked from melted snow and a nearby spider was twitching like it was waking from a deep sleep.

We didn't have much time.

"Fine-then," Oti agreed. "Now-repeat-after-me." She exhaled slowly and spread her arms. Her words were chanted in the sing-song voice she'd used before.

Princess Oti, I believe
Princess-power can save me—

"I'm not saying that!" I roared at her.

Oti laughed and spun around on her toes like an ice skater.

C-r-i-i-i-c-k, came a sharp splitting noise and we froze.

"Never-mind!" Oti shouted. "Just-start-climbing. I-will-get-us-up."

I wasn't all that confident, but we didn't have a choice. It was either climb or face the spiders again.

Simon and Oti raced to the funnel and started up. I was about to do the same when I realized the hammer was still frozen to my hands.

I couldn't climb with it stuck there!

Crick! The last of the ice split apart from the closest spider. The beast was free.

And I was trapped.

My friends were climbing above me, my back was to the funnel web, and the hammer had shrunk to the size of a serving spoon.

The shard spider's heartbeat flashed wickedly as it advanced.

Back to Burrowfar

36

The shard spider clicked its mandibles together and stalked toward me. I'm not sure if the creature was smart enough to make a battle plan, but it looked like it was sizing me up. Its red gaze burned fiercely.

I hoped it wasn't smart enough to realize I didn't have a weapon anymore.

I crouched and watched the spider carefully. Just my luck, it was bigger than most of the others. More like a small pony than a big dog.

Clack-clack went its mandibles. It was almost on top of me.

"Connor-Gnomefriend!" Princess Oti cried from above and behind me.

The spider stopped and that was as far as it ever got. I glanced over my shoulder in time to see Oti draw in a deep breath. She was hanging from the funnel web by one hand and foot.

Her tiny, round face reddened as she shrieked at the spider.

E-E-E-Y-A-A-H!

With the sound of a roaring wind, the spider exploded.

Then my hammer shattered, too, and I flew backward and crashed into the web. Slush and mud soaked my clothes where I landed.

That was a powerful blast. I hadn't heard the princess roar so loudly before. She'd shattered spiders but never knocked me off my feet.

"Hurry, Connor!" This time it was Simon shouting down at me. "More spiders are coming."

I struggled to get over my shock and rubbed my eyes. There were shapes moving in the mist just ahead.

I didn't wait to see them clearly. I jumped to my feet and climbed. The crossed strands of crystal made the web almost as easy to climb as a ladder.

In seconds, I reached Simon and Oti. The princess was panting, her face red, and Simon's eyes were wide.

"They're starting to climb," he warned us urgently. "At least six of them. We have to get moving."

Oti was still breathing hard. I guess using magic made her tired the same way it made Simon tired.

Knowing that made me glad I was good with a sword.

"Can you climb?" I asked Oti.

She tried to smile but the corners of her mouth barely twitched. "A-princess-can-always-climb," she wheezed.

I knew right away that she was lying. She was exhausted but would never admit it. If she tried to go any farther, she'd fall to the rocky island below.

That left helping Oti up to me.

"Climb onto my back," I told her. "I'm going to carry you piggyback."

For a brief moment, Oti's eyes flashed then faded. She'd wanted to argue with me, I could tell.

Lucky for us she was too tired. Lucky for me she was so little and light.

Panting and moving cautiously, she scooted across the funnel to me and wrapped her arms around my neck.

"Ready?" I asked when she'd quit wiggling and seemed comfortable.

"Ready, Sir-Connor-Gnomefriend," she whispered quietly, "and-thank-you."

I tried to shrug but couldn't with her on my back. It was an honor to help her. She'd done the same for me and I owed her.

But most of all, she was my friend. I would never leave a friend in danger.

To Thank, Keep, or Earn a Friend, Be One Faithfully, read Act Sixty of the *Noble Deeds and Duties.*

"The spiders are halfway up," Simon warned.

"Let's go then," I said and started to climb.

"Gee, good idea," he replied sarcastically as he scampered up.

I didn't look down as we climbed. It wasn't the height or the thought of falling. It was knowing that we had to reach the top. That *I* had to reach the top.

If I didn't make it, neither would Simon and Oti. Simon had already slipped and crashed into me. Had I not been beneath him, who knows how far he'd have fallen.

As for Princess Oti, she was still too weak to climb. I know she'd planned to help us with magic, but she couldn't. She needed to recover her strength.

So I climbed while Oti clutched my neck and Simon clumsily clawed his way up above me. I climbed without stopping or slowing until my arms ached with fatigue.

I'm not sure how long it took, but when we reached the top, I collapsed onto the floor. Sweat covered my whole body.

We'd climbed up through a narrow crack into a small, damp room. At first I thought it was a dungeon cell, but the door didn't have any bars or lock.

"What is this place?" I murmured.

"Burrowfar," Oti whispered like a prayer. "I-have-come-home."

A shiver crept up my spine as I stared at the door. Somewhere beyond it Nebbezim waited for us.

Secret Suspicions

37

"Listen-closely," Oti said with a quick glance to the door, "because-I-will-not-be-able-to-repeat-myself." Her words were hushed but they still echoed in the small room.

Even though it was a silly idea, I worried that Nebbezim would hear her.

We were in Burrowfar again. Back with the living dead. Back with Nebbezim. Who knew what magic lurked about?

"This-is-the-lowest-level-of-the-castle," Oti continued. She was talking slowly for her, but her words were still fast. "When-we-leave-here, I-will-not-be-able-to-speak-again."

She didn't need to explain any more than that. I remembered the tiny statues Simon and I had seen. The tiny gnomes that had been turned to stone.

Nebbezim had put a curse on Castle Burrowfar and the gnomes. If a gnome spoke inside the castle, he or she would be petrified. *Petrified* means turned to stone.

Because of the curse, Oti wouldn't be able to talk inside

the castle or use her magic against Nebbezim. Defeating the necromancer would be up to me and Simon.

"Keep your pockets unbuttoned," I told Simon. I wanted the ingredients for his spells easy to reach.

He nodded his shaggy head and smiled bravely. Peasant or not, Simon was all right.

"I-will-lead," Oti squeaked, "but-you-must-follow-closely-and-quickly. Burrowfar-is-quite-large-and-it-is-a-long-way-to-Nebbezim's-tower."

Suddenly a suspicious thought struck me.

A long way to Nebbezim's tower, Oti had said.

How could she possibly know that? No gnome had been inside Castle Burrowfar for hundreds of years.

Wondering that, my thoughts grew dark. Maybe the princess was leading us into some sort of trap. Maybe the gnomes had been sent underground for a reason.

How much did we really know about Princess Oti and her people anyway?

I glanced at Simon without moving my head. I didn't want Oti to notice me looking.

But if Simon was thinking the same as me, he didn't show it. He was concentrating on adjusting his robes for battle.

I'd have to keep my suspicions quiet for a while.

"Now-let-us-go," Oti chirped and her purple eyes shone fiercely. "Remember, please, to-follow-closely."

Very closely, I agreed silently. I planned on keeping my eyes on her, watching for tricks or traps.

Oti led us out of the room and into a narrow black passage. Away from the glowing funnel web, there was no light anywhere. Simon and I bumped into each other right away.

"Wait," he said almost directly into my ear. He shuffled back a step and whispered words I didn't understand.

A blue light flared and then dimmed to the familiar glowing ball he'd conjured before. It floated just above his open palm. "All right, I'm ready," he said.

Oti nodded then continued down the passage without a sound. Her pace was straight and fast.

Simon and I followed with the blue light surrounding us. I tried to lag behind so that I could whisper to him privately, but Oti noticed and waited for us to catch up.

It made me want to scream in frustration. I couldn't warn Simon about Oti.

It didn't take long for me to feel lost. Princess Oti turned down passages, climbed stairs, and went through doors without hesitating. She seemed confident in which way to go.

How suspicious, I thought.

I couldn't be sure, but I got the idea that Oti was trying to confuse us in the castle's maze-like passages. Like she wanted us lost before springing her trap.

But that didn't happen. Instead, we rounded a corner and stumbled right into a pair of sweating goblins. They were breathing hard and in a hurry.

"Outta da way!" one of them bellowed. He wore a black eyepatch and I recognized him as Goblin Champion Schrat.

One of the goblins that had tried to kill us!

Outta da Way!

38

Goblin Champion Schrat!

We were in more trouble than I'd thought.

"It's Schrat!" I cried in warning.

Oti didn't know who Schrat was, but Simon did. He grabbed her arm and pulled her back with us.

For several seconds, no one moved.

The goblins stared at us. We stared at the goblins. Tense silence filled the hallway.

Finally Schrat hissed and flailed his knobby arms at us. "Me said outta da way. We gots no beef wit you."

Like I was going to believe that. Schrat and his goblin pal had chased us into Burrowfar. They were Sir Filabard's henchmen.

"You tried to kill us," I said coldly.

Schrat waved a green hand at me. "Dat's old news. We isn't workin' fer da knight anymo'."

Not working for Sir Filabard?

That was a good surprise, but I doubted it was true. It sounded like a goblin trick.

"Then what are you doing here?" Simon challenged. He'd read my thoughts exactly.

"Leavin'," Schrat growled. "Dat knight is crazy. He be makin' nice wit a talkin' skull."

Nebbezim!

Simon and I gasped at the same time. Sir Filabard had already reached Nebbezim's tower. We were too late.

"Now gets outta da way or we do gots a beef wit you," Schrat warned. He grinned, showing rows of sharp yellow teeth.

There wasn't any reason to stop the goblins, so we let them go. We didn't need another fight just then.

"Watch where you go, princess" I warned Oti after the goblins had scrambled down the hall. I meant she should be careful of trying to trick me and Simon.

She glanced at me curiously, then shrugged and started down the passage again.

Good, I thought as I watched her go. *She knows I'm onto her*.

I winked at Simon but he frowned in response. He obviously hadn't discovered Oti's secret yet.

I'd tell him when the time was right.

Up some wide steps and through a square blue door, we came to a familiar hallway. The memories were hazy in my mind, but I knew we'd been there before.

It was the hall leading to Nebbezim's tower.

The petrified gnome statues stood exactly where they'd been during our first visit. According to Oti, they hadn't moved in over eight hundred years.

Oti's shoulders shook as she walked past the stone gnomes. When she reached the carved door to the tower, she turned to face me and Simon. There were tears in her eyes and on her cheeks.

"Are you…?" Simon started to ask but stopped when Oti held up a shaky hand. She couldn't speak, so there was no point to asking questions.

The princess pointed at the heavy door and made a pushing motion. Simon and I would have to open it. Oti wasn't big or strong enough to do it.

We nodded and moved up to throw our shoulders against the door. As we pushed, I realized it was the time for action.

Nebbezim and Sir Filabard were in the tower, and Princess Oti was planning a trap.

It was time for Simon and me to go on alone. We'd have enough trouble inside the tower without worrying about Oti.

Finally the door creaked open far enough for us to wiggle through. I stepped back and pointed slowly at myself, then Simon, then Oti. We would go through the door in that order.

At least that's what I wanted them to think.

They nodded in understanding, so I took a deep breath and squeezed into the tower. Musty darkness and the scent of death filled my nostrils.

I didn't wait for Simon to get all the way inside. When his arm and shoulder appeared in the doorway, I grabbed his robes and hauled him through.

"What was that for?" he asked in shock, but I didn't answer.

I did something horrible instead. Something no knight should ever have done.

I threw my weight against the door and slammed it shut.

Princess Oti, the girl who had saved my life at least twice, was trapped outside the tower.

Hourglasses Everywhere

39

"Why did you do that?" Simon roared in accusation. "Are you crazy?"

I couldn't believe I'd done it either. I'd trapped Oti on the other side of the door. But I'd had my reasons. I just hoped they were good ones.

"Help me open the door," Simon demanded. "We need her. We can't leave her out there."

Simon tried to push his way past me. His angry face was almost the same color as his hair.

"No," I told him.

"*No*?" he repeated, still trying to get around me. "Some knight you are."

That made me angry. Simon's words hurt because they were true. I wasn't behaving at all like a knight.

Never Betray the Trust of Others, Act Two of the *Noble Deeds and Duties* said, but I'd done that and worse. I'd betrayed the trust of a friend.

But was Princess Oti really a friend?

I was so confused that I just became angrier. I didn't know what to think.

So I didn't.

"Listen, peasant," I growled. "She was going to trick us. How do you think she could lead us through this castle? Gnomes haven't been here for hundreds of years."

Simon groaned and rolled his eyes. "You really have gone crazy! The gnome palace in Deephome-Glimmering looks exactly like this."

I felt suddenly dizzy. I'd forgotten about New Burrowfar.

"But what about this tower?" I pressed. "She knew right where to go. How many towers does a castle have?"

That point made Simon stop struggling to get around me. He knew the castle had many towers. What were the odds of Oti picking the right one on the first try?

He thought for a moment. "All right," he said at last. "We'll handle Nebbezim ourselves. Oti will be safe outside until we're done here."

Aaaahhhhhh.

A long sigh came from behind us. It sounded like an ancient tomb opening for the first time in a thousand years.

We turned to see Sir Filabard on the stairs across the room. He glided down the steps without his feet touching the floor. On one hand he wore his jeweled ring. In the other he gripped some sort of large crystal key. It looked to be made of the same crystal found in Deephome-

Glimmering.

A flock of undead ravens flapped and cawed from over his shoulder. Their stench blasted our faces like a zombie's sucker punch.

Behind them, two armored figures huddled on the stairs.

But where were the birdcage and Nebbezim?

"I'm afraid...*aid*," Sir Filabard hissed in a haunting echo, "that you are done now...*ow*."

That voice! It was Nebbezim's. Sir Filabard was talking in Nebbezim's voice.

Then Sir Filabard turned his eyes on us, and Simon and I shrank back in despair. His eyes weren't human anymore. They were red, blazing fire.

And shaped like hourglasses.

I knew immediately what had happened. Nebbezim wasn't waiting up the stairs. He was *inside* Sir Filabard. The two had somehow become the same person. The same *thing*.

Sir Filabard raised his hand and his bloody ring flashed. "Destroy the intruders...*ers*," he commanded.

The pair of armored figures on the stairs shuffled forward woodenly like puppets without knees or elbows.

But they weren't skeletons. They were our fathers.

Their faces were blank and hourglasses shone in their eyes.

To Find a Hero

40

"Father!" I cried.

"Dad!" wailed Simon.

Our fathers were under Sir Filabard's control more than ever before. They didn't seem to recognize us. Their dead eyes stared at nothing.

They grabbed us roughly by the shoulders and started dragging us toward the stairs. We couldn't bring ourselves to struggle against them. They were our fathers!

Sir Filabard cackled hollowly, sounding more and more like Nebbezim. "You sought to defy…*fy* me, children. You must be punished…*ished*. It's back to the deep for you."

His chilling words followed us up the stairs, their meaning becoming more frightening with every step.

We were going to be dropped out the tower's window.

By our fathers.

This time we wouldn't have Simon's spells or magic feathers to protect us. We'd fall like rocks to the cavern floor.

After outrunning goblins, escaping Nebbezim's tower, meeting the gnomes, crossing Fleshfeast Flood, and battling shard spiders, we were doomed.

We'd done everything we could, but it hadn't been enough. Sir Filabard and Nebbezim were going to win. They—he—whichever Sir Filabard was—had beaten us.

Simon and I had failed.

We'd failed as pages, as knights, and as students of the *Noble Deeds and Duties*. We'd—

The *Noble Deeds and Duties*!

How could I have forgotten them and one of the most important Acts at such a time?

Act One. *To Find a Hero, Look into a Mirror*.

Everyone could be a hero. Me, Simon, Princess Oti, Mr. Sootbeard the blacksmith, Enu the Foregnome. Everyone.

Being a hero doesn't take muscles, spells, or gold. It takes heart and the desire to do what is right. Everyone in the world has those things.

I knew Simon and I did.

And we weren't about to give up.

At the top of the stairs we heard a loud crash from below. It sounded like a tree snapping and splitting apart.

My father paused at the noise and I glanced over my shoulder to see him shake his head in confusion like he was waking from a bad dream.

"C-Connor…?" he mumbled drowsily.

My hopes soared. "It's me, father! It's Connor!" I exclaimed.

Then Sir Filabard appeared suddenly before us like a ghost. His hourglass eyes burned so brightly they were hard to look at.

He raised his hand and the red ring on his finger pulsed with a sinister light. "Obey your master...*ster*," he demanded.

I felt my father's body relax like he'd fallen asleep, but his grip on my shoulders tightened.

Sir Filabard's ring was controlling him, I realized. Somehow the scruffy knight used it to hypnotize people.

With heavy steps, my father began marching toward the window again. He was back under Sir Filabard's control and there was nothing I could do about it.

Petrified

41

Sir Filabard glided like mist down the hall to the tower's window. There he rotated slowly around. Nebbezim's empty birdcage lay at his feet.

"We must thank you, boy...*oy*, for the horse," he smirked at me. "We could not have reached the Turning of the Pages without...*out* it."

He meant Honormark, my stallion. He'd stolen him from Mr. Sootbeard's stable.

"Honormark wasn't a gift," I spat.

Sir Filabard smiled and let out a ghostly sigh. "Nevertheless, it is a fine animal...*mal*. Nothing like those dreadful worms below."

He glanced out the window and idly toyed with the crystal key in his hand. "We should exterminate them and the bothersome gnomes, too. They—"

"Why-not-start-with-me?" challenged a familiar rapid voice.

It was Princess Oti! She'd managed to get past the door and speak inside the castle. Had she forgotten the curse or figured some way around it?

Her footsteps were loud and heavy, but I'd never been so happy to see anyone. Until I got a good look at her, that is.

Oti's feet and legs were stone. To walk, she had to sway back and forth, pivoting from leg to leg. Her knees and ankles couldn't bend.

Sir Filabard took one look at her and burst out laughing. "Put on some weight, princess...*cess*?" he cackled.

Grimacing, Oti raised one arm and pointed at him. "You-will-pay-for-what-you-have-done-to-my-people," she threatened.

A crackling sound like paper being crushed into a ball echoed through the tower. As I watched, Oti's raised arm stiffened and darkened.

Talking had turned it to stone!

I hated to see her like that, but I couldn't think about it then. None of us had much time.

"The ring, Oti!" I cried. "Destroy the ring!" I was counting on her magic.

Luckily she understood.

E-E-E-Y-A-A-H! she screamed and Sir Filabard yelped in pain as the hourglass ring on his finger flashed and exploded into a twinkling red dust.

He threw down the key he'd been holding and grasped his injured hand.

A blazing glow filled the tower then quickly faded. When I looked again, Oti was completely petrified. Her whole body, clothes and all, were frozen.

"Oti!" Simon cried, but she couldn't answer or even hear. She was gone.

But her magic had worked like I'd hoped it would. Our fathers were free of the ring's power.

They came out of their trances and dropped us to the floor. With blinding speed they drew swords from the scabbards on their hips.

"Stay back!" my father ordered and charged Sir Filabard. Simon's father ran right behind him.

Cradling his wounded hand, Sir Filabard met their attack. He waved his good hand in front of his chest and moaned the words to a short spell.

Be rock, be stone—
Your flesh, your bone!

A muddy haze swelled from his hand and floated toward our fathers. When it touched them, they stopped moving and were petrified instantly.

They didn't have time to dodge or cry out. With the crackling sound we'd heard earlier, they were turned to stone.

Deep silence followed.

Simon and I were alone and helpless. Oti was stone. Our

fathers were statues. We had no weapons.

How could we hope to defeat Sir Filabard?

The Key to Victory

42

Still clutching his injured hand, Sir Filabard slumped against the window ledge. His breath was quick and shallow.

He looked and sounded like Simon after he'd used too much magic. Like Oti after our battle with the shard spiders.

He looked tired.

"There is still a matter of your punishment, children...*ren*," he wheezed weakly, and I knew I was right.

Sir Filabard was exhausted. The destruction of his ring. Turning our fathers to stone. Those events had weakened him.

If we attacked, we might have a chance.

"Now, Simon!" I roared, leaping to my feet. I hoped he understood what I expected. I wanted him to pull something amazing from the pockets of his robe before Sir Filabard recovered.

At the top of his lungs, Simon shouted:

Now fly, I cry,
O crystal key!
Defy, says I,
All gravity!

He threw out his hands at Sir Filabard's fallen key. Spinning slowly, it floated into the air and levitated toward him.

What are you doing? I wanted to scream. I'd hoped he'd cast a sizzling fireball or an earthquake, not perform a useless magic trick.

Why couldn't he have cast something else? Wizards were supposed to shoot lightning from their eyes, weren't they?

Before the floating key reached Simon's extended fingers, Sir Filabard smirked. "You have talent, young wizard...*ard*, but much to learn. Observe:

Whisper, drawl,
Mutter, roar—
Cease them all.
Speak no more!

As soon as he finished chanting, the crystal key dropped to the floor and Simon's eyes widened in terror.

Something terrible was happening.

Simon's hands flew to his face.

His mouth was completely gone. His lips had vanished and solid skin stretched from his chin to his nose.

He'd sacrificed everything to get the crystal key. But why?

Sir Filabard watched with amusement as Simon struggled on the floor. The scruffy knight was enjoying himself. He ignored everything but Simon. Me, the statues, the birdcage, the crystal—

The birdcage and the crystal key.

That was it! I knew why Simon had tried to take the key.

He wanted to lock Sir Filabard in the birdcage.

Act Seventy of the *Noble Deeds and Duties* popped into my head:

Imagination is a Knight's Right Hand.

As usual, Simon had remembered and understood the Act. He'd realized that the birdcage and key were our only weapons.

Sir Filabard strutted toward Simon, chuckling the way a bully gloats over a smaller kid who's been pushed down.

He didn't notice me until I'd snatched up the fallen key. When he did, I immediately dove toward the cage next.

"What—?" he hissed at me and brought up his hands.

He was casting a spell, but I couldn't stop. I was a page, a knight, and a hero. It was time for me to prove it.

I hit the floor with a grunt and rolled. The birdcage skipped away from my sweaty fingers, clattering noisily over the stones.

"Be rock, be stone..." Sir Filabard chanted tiredly. His voice was weak and slow.

But I was a bolt of lightning from a wizard's eye.

I threw myself at the birdcage again and my fingers speared through its bars, tightening into a strong fist.

The cage was mine.

"Your flesh!" Sir Filabard shrieked, the pitch of his voice rising sharply.

I slammed the crystal key into the birdcage's lock and clawed open the tiny door. Then I spun around with the cage held before me like a shield.

Sir Filabard spotted me with the opened birdcage and wailed. "Your—Nooo!"

"Sir Filabard," I roared, "you're no knight! You're just a peasant!"

Sir Filabard wasn't even human. *It* was an undead nightmare that needed to be destroyed. Whatever had been the real Sir Filabard was gone.

"Not again!" he moaned chillingly as dark light surrounded his hands in a funnel shape that stretched from the open door of the birdcage.

He was being sucked inside.

The funnel of light grew larger, drawing more of Sir Filabard into its radiance. Wherever it touched him, he faded into tiny bits and seeped into the cage like sand pouring through an hourglass.

Somehow that was fitting.

When the light faded, Sir Filabard was gone and I slapped the birdcage's door closed. I didn't look inside. I didn't want to see what was there.

Instead, I tore the key from the lock and hurled the cage out of the tower's window. I'd thought the nightmare was over.

Whoosh!

A mass of black shapes whipped by my head and out the window. The stench of their passing took my breath away.

As I watched them go, the tower suddenly rumbled beneath my feet.

G-R-R-R-E-N-D-T-C-H, it thrashed violently.

When floor rumbled again, it shook the walls and ceiling, too. Dust and bits of stone rained down on my head. I tried to get to my feet but slipped.

My head hit the floor and darkness filled my eyes.

Re-Turning

43

When I opened my eyes, I squeezed them shut again right away. Bright sunlight filled the room.

"Wake-up, Sir-Connor-Lay-About," a speedy voice chirped happily.

It sounded like Princess Oti.

I carefully opened my eyes. Cheery purple eyes stared back at me.

"Oti!" I exclaimed excitedly, sitting straight up.

She was kneeling on the foot of my bed. Simon sat next to her. Both of them were munching fresh apples.

"Good morning, sir," Simon winked, taking a crunchy bite.

I didn't know how to respond. *Good morning* just didn't seem like enough. I had so many questions.

"Where are we?" I finally blurted at Simon. "How did you get changed back?" I asked Oti.

My stomach rumbled, so I added "Have any more

apples?"

Oti and Simon laughed at me, but not in a mean way. They seemed as glad to see me as I was to see them.

I couldn't believe that we were all alive and safe. Simon's mouth had reappeared and Oti wasn't a statue.

Simon pulled an apple from a pocket, shined it on his robe, then tossed it to me. I caught it and started to take a bite, but my hand froze halfway to my mouth.

Where was my father? He'd been turned to stone, too.

"My father?" I asked quietly, dreading the response.

Oti answered in an excited rush. "He-went-to-find-my-father-so-that-he-could-thank-you. He-is-very-eager-to-see-you-again."

King Ogogiyargo? What was he doing here—wherever here was?

I groaned and flopped back down on my pillow. "Will someone please tell me what's going on?" At least I knew my father was safe.

Oti leaped to her feet and started to bounce around on the bed. "You-saved-us, Connor-Gnomefriend. You-saved-my-people-from-Nebbezim-and-his-terrible-curses."

Suddenly she hopped to the floor, bent down, and kissed me on the forehead. "On-behalf-of-the-gnomes-of-Burrowfar, I, Princess-Otoonuoti, thank-you." Her smile was huge.

Speechless, I stared up at her. The wheels in my mind were churning. Something about what she'd said surprised me.

Burrowfar, not *New* Burrowfar. That meant....

"We're still in the castle, aren't we?" I said. It was a question but I already knew the answer.

"That-is-right," Oti beamed.

"After you threw Sir Filabard...Lord Nebbezim...*it* out the window," Simon explained slowly, "all the curses evaporated. The castle rose to the surface and the statues came back to life."

I couldn't resist teasing him. "You got your mouth back, too. Think that's a good thing?" It was my turn to smile.

He wiggled his fingers at me and was about to say something when there came a knock on the door. My father entered followed by King Ogogiyargo of the gnomes.

I flew out of bed and dashed right by King Ogo. I crashed into my father and gave him a huge hug.

There were lots of kings in the world, but I only had one father. The *Noble Deeds and Duties* didn't mention anything about that, but it should. Act One Hundred and One could go something like:

Honor Kings and Queens But Love Thy Family Most of All.

Besides, I wasn't an official knight yet. I could still get away with misbehaving a little bit.

Everyone in the room laughed, especially King Ogo. He

had a daughter, so I guessed he understood family.

"Greetings-again, Sir-Connor-Gnomefriend," he chirped with a tug on his beard. "Welcome-to-Burrowfar-and-many-thank-yous. We-gnomes-have-waited-over-eight-hundred-years-to-return-to-our-home."

As I listened to him, something important dawned on me. I whipped my head around to look at Oti.

"Just how old are you?" I asked. It sounded almost like an accusation.

Oti wasn't offended. "Next-month-I-will-turn-nine-hundred-three," she giggled. Then she added "I-am-afraid-I-am-much-too-old-to-be-your-girlfriend."

I ignored her second comment as what she'd told me sank in. Nine hundred and three years old. That's how she'd known all about Nebbezim and could lead us to his tower. She'd lived in the real Burrowfar before Nebbezim had put his curses on the gnomes and their home.

Princess Oti wasn't a traitor. She was my friend. I shouldn't have forgotten that.

Boy, did I feel like a dolt.

"I'm sor—" I started to apologize lamely, but she turned and skipped to an open window.

"Glimmers, come-see-what-I-see!" she squeaked.

I glanced from my father to King Ogo to Simon. They all smiled and nodded, so I joined Oti by the window.

We were quite high up but not in a tower. For some reason I was glad for that. Sunshine warmed a large grassy valley below.

It took me a minute to recognize it, but we were overlooking the valley where Sir Filabard had ordered us to set up camp. Where Simon and I had first encountered Goblin Champion Schrat.

Those things seemed so long ago.

The valley looked very different. Tents, banners, and flags flapped slowly in a pleasant breeze. Horses grazed freely. Humans and gnomes scurried about. There was even a napping slithersaur curled up in the sunshine.

Seeing everything reminded me of a festival. The way Battledown Yard had looked when I'd seen it last.

"The Turning of the Pages," my father said proudly from behind me. "Today you become a knight."

My jaw dropped. Could it finally be true? It would explain the decorations and activity in the valley.

Simon stood by the door. "Let's go!" he urged.

I didn't have to be asked twice. I sprinted across the room.

"Race you there, peasant!" I shouted as I shot through the door.

The End

Be sure to visit:

www.knightscares.com

For the latest conjurings and spells from the co-wizards of Knightscares.

Invite the Co-Authors to Visit Your School

Preview Upcoming Adventures

Join the Knightscares Fan Club

Write Your Own Review

Meet the Writers

Calling All Artists

The wizards at Knightscares are interested in seeing YOUR drawings of your favorite Knightscares characters.

Some drawings will even be selected to appear in future Knightscares books. Others will be added to our website for everyone to enjoy.

If your drawing is selected to appear in a future book, we will send you a free, autographed copy of the book with your drawing and name in it.

Send your drawings to:

Sigil Publishing
Knightscares Artwork
P.O. Box 824
Leland, Michigan 49654

Please include your name, age, and address (or email) so that we can contact you!

Feel free to draw any character you'd like from any Knightscares adventure.

Knightscares #3
Early Winter's Orb

Emily expects nothing but fun during the fall's annual Celebration of Leaves. Along with her parents and the family dog, a playful giant named Leland, she travels into town in the hopes of winning the Sling and Archery competition for the 13-year old age group.

But at the festival, things start to go terribly wrong. A deep, unnatural snow blankets the town, and the waters of the Longrapid River begin to flow backward.

When a strange rider arrives to tell a tale of snow beasts come down from the mountains, it's up to Emily, Leland, and their friend Daniel to save the land from endless winter.

Knightscares #3: Early Winter's Orb
Coming October 2003

Visit www.knightscares.com for details.

Knightscares Sleuth

Use the clues below to fill the blanks on the following page.
Once you do, you'll know the answer to this question:

Opal is the name of a *what*?

(1) Name of the blacksmith. *Mr.*?

(2) A nasty creature with green skin and a big head.

(3) Nebbezim is trapped in one.

(4) Connor has always wanted to be this.

(5) Type of sword Connor finds in the armory.

(6) Simon juggles this kind of fruit.

(7) Name of Connor's horse.

(8) The Goblin Champion.

(9) The name Connor calls Simon.

(10) Name of the first gnome Connor and Simon meet.

(11) Name of the blacksmith's dog.

Knightscares Sleuth

Opal is the name of a *what*?

(1) ☐ _ _ _ _ _ _ _ _

(2) _ _ _ ☐ _ _

(3) _ ☐ _ _ _ _ _ _

(4) _ _ _ _ _ ☐

(5) _ _ _ _ ☐ _ _ _

(6) _ _ _ _ ☐

(7) _ _ _ _ ☐ _ _ _ _

(8) ☐ _ _ _ _ _

(9) _ _ ☐ _ _ _ _

(10) _ _ ☐

(11) _ _ _ ☐ _

Skull in the Birdcage Wordsearch

T B H O U L G S A R A M T I J A S I A H
U R U A S R E H T I L S F C O N M R O C
H N S T L I F I L A B A R D U E Y P T E
O H B I D C A J W E C I O N S A N T P A
N O O C H A R L I E M E S N T K U L R L
K S K N E B B E Z I M A K I D A V I D B
R J I M O D A G F P L G E R M C O L M E
A C A S T R N Y Z E R N L D I O L I P Y
S E P O E T M J L R E O E R D S N N R E
Q X L W R S I A N F N M T I A G T E I S
P I O L G A R P R B T E O Z D R A E N N
H T B I W I A P P K H M N E T A G O C O
J O I G D Z R L A L L A U R A N U N E L
R W R I O H L E G A R I S M F I L A S O
F R D S H E A L M I O N C H A P D L S C
G E C A L H E N C H M A N U L K W D A D
A R A F B I M O L E C C I S C A I A L E
P G G K N I G E Y E P A T C H D T R G L
L R E D I P S P P I A H A T I Z K F R V
P P U N O R W I N A G E L O O E C M U A
E L E B R A N D T T E N I P N G I N O H
R I L G C O N N O R K I D T H E R M H L
I C K N I S C Q U O R L I S K C A R E L
N A A R N G O V Y N C P E A S A N T C G
C N T E P A H M E U S E N G S L T I H U

Apple	Joust
Birdcage	Nebbezim
Connor	Page
Eyepatch	Peasant
Falchion	Princess
Filabard	Simon
Gnome	Skeleton
Henchman	Slithersaur
Honormark	Spider
Hourglass	Tower